Praise for *Of Fathe*

"They say Jacob wrestled with the Lord; writers like Jim Roberts continue that tradition of spiritual grappling. *Of Fathers & Gods* is an auspicious debut, nine stories that will pin you every time."

—**Aaron Gwyn, author of** *All God's Children* **and** *Wynne's War*

"From the first story (loaded with grief, guts, and grit) to the last (unforgiving with tongue-in-cheek), *Of Fathers & Gods* provokes as much as it coaxes. Characters have sharp edges that Roberts uses to trim up his stories. Every once in a while they nick, or even slice into you. The words he wraps them in are surgical in their precision. Whether the setting is downtown Brooklyn or a lazy Texas river, Roberts creates atmospheres intricate enough to bury family secrets. Men populating the book are the fathers you know—some you wish you didn't. With them Roberts asks old questions but offers fresh answers from cover to cover: What do gods make of fathers? What gods do fathers make?"

—**Toby LeBlanc, author of** *Dark Roux*

"Jim Roberts writes with truth and clarity. Each searing story gets to the heart of humanity. A collection you'll devour and then go back to for seconds."

—**Mark Westmoreland, author of** *A Violent Gospel* **and**
A Mourning Song

"These are stories haunted by father figures, both present and passed, and by the many ways they've failed their children. Through stories about kidnapping, prosthesis creation, family secrets and mass shootings, Roberts never loses sight of the thumping, bleeding hearts of his characters, yearning for better lives. If you're looking for the firm, no-nonsense truths of Flannery O'Connor and the raw, hardscrabble edge of Denis Johnson, this is your book. You would be wise to pick up a copy."

—**John Matthew Fox, founder of Bookfox and**
author of *I Will Shout Your Name*

Of Fathers & Gods

BELLE
POINT
PRESS

Fort Smith, Arkansas

Of Fathers & Gods

Stories

Jim Roberts

OF FATHERS & GODS

Edited by Casie Dodd
Cover elements via Canva Pro license
Cover design by Casie Dodd
Author photo by Mark Roberts
Title set in Albertan Pro
Text set in Arno Pro

Belle Point Press, LLC
Fort Smith, Arkansas
bellepointpress.com
editor@bellepointpress.com

Find Belle Point Press
on Facebook, Substack,
and Instagram (@bellepointpress)

Printed in the United States of America

28 27 26 25 24   1 2 3 4 5

Library of Congress Control Number: 2024933292

ISBN: 978-1-960215-15-4

OFG/BPP27

In memory of my father,
Roy Dee Roberts.
The best man I ever knew.
And Dad, to answer your famous question:
Yes indeed, I do have a frog in my pocket. Always.
It's you.

Contents

While Her Guitar Gently Weeps

I DON'T TALK to Mariela's ghost, sitting in a chair against the wall, brushing her long black hair and humming "Imagine." If her face appears in my coffee, I milk it out. If I hear our baby crying in the middle of the night, I don't whisper "I'll get him" and stumble down the hall for fatherly duty.

There is no baby, no Joey, the name we pick the day we run through a downpour to our car, sonogram photos in a gray hospital envelope tucked in my jacket. We sit in the car, drenched and howling with delight, inspecting the magical images. *Look, an ear. An ear for God's sake! A mouth, a nose, a little pecker.* Mariela is convinced it's a girl, and we'll name her Joy. But the pecker puts an end to that, so Joy turns into Joey.

We are in no hurry to end this glorious moment, so we talk and kiss and fog up the windows, listen to the rain turn into hail and mercilessly beat our car. A tornado watch lights up our phones, and we cackle at how neither of us can remember the difference between a *watch* and a *warning*. One's bullshit; the other kills you. We laugh at everything on this treasure of a day. We are twenty-five and invincible and so dangerously close to happy.

* * *

No one expects to die at Kroger. The media ran the surveillance footage over and over for days right after. Me pushing our cart, and Mariela, eight months pregnant, walking ahead. A dreck of a man shooting down each aisle. Mariela stooped over, reaching for a taco kit. Her body raking across the shelves before sprawling on the floor amidst a chaos of cans and boxes.

Me? Not charging him. Not running the cart at him. Not throwing my body over her. Them.

The camera sees all this, but it can't see me praying. Praying to my parents' God, the God of twice on Sunday and every Wednesday night and Vacation Bible School, summer after summer, a God I shunned since puberty. It's a cruel way to learn the truth of Granddad's cliche: *Ain't no atheists in foxholes.*

What the camera doesn't miss is me ducking behind the cart, hiding and covering my head, curling up like a worm and letting a motherfucker murder my family without a fight. The world doesn't miss that:

Punk-ass p**sy coward—Hotdaddy45.

Bet that bro shit hisself—ScatmanTX.

Hey hidey-hole guy, warm & cmfy over there?—ZacTheRat

Dozens of bullets fly, but only one hits her. One fucking bullet. Mariela bleeds out before the police can arrive and take down the shooter. Joey's heart stops five miles from the hospital. Not a scratch on me.

That single bullet's a marvel of physics, a cosmic cleaving force, dividing time into before and after. Before, I had a life. After, I breathe and eat and move around between points A and B, and they don't, so in that sense I live. And they don't. *They don't.*

I'm alive, but I don't have a life. I pantomime one.

*   *   *

People think I have a job. Funny thing: if you stop going to work, they stop paying you. Who knew? You lose your little two-bedroom starter home. One night a shaggy guy with a barbed-wire tattoo around his neck tows your car off.

My landlady, Glenda Sloan, thinks I still have a job. She calls herself Ducky. I owe Ducky three months' back rent, but she hasn't mentioned it. I live in her attic. Ducky's late husband Rob converted it into a studio apartment a decade ago, when he was dying, to provide extra income after he was gone. Guess I'm screwing up Dead Rob's plan.

I try to sneak out past Ducky. Not just because of the overdue rent. Once she grabs me, it's almost impossible to break away. She wants to sit and have coffee. She wants me to replace some light bulbs she can't reach. Open a jar of olives. Figure out why her Wi-Fi is down. Wants me to wear Dead Rob's clothes.

"He had a lot of nice suits. It'd be a shame to burn them. Your generation doesn't dress for work like men used to," she says.

"Or you could give them to Goodwill," I say as I slip my arms into a navy pinstripe suitcoat she holds up.

"Perfect fit!" Ducky beams. "You remind me so much of Rob when he was your age."

I can't escape because Dead Rob's clothes do fit well, so she loads me up with a pile of suits and enough dress shirts and silk ties to open a haberdashery.

*   *   *

In the mornings, when she catches me leaving for my pretend job, sharply dressed, we "must have" breakfast. More likely, we just drink coffee. Well, I have coffee and she has coffee with gin. Ducky buys it by the gallon and mixes it with anything. *Anything*. She calls her drinks *ginevers*, gin with what*ever* is handy. Coffee. Tea. Apple juice. Gatorade. Clam juice. I swear to God she put it in prune juice one morning.

*   *   *

I step off the bus near the downtown library, my hangout most days, and hear a brassy voice urging anyone in earshot to accept Christ. She goes by "Mary," but all the people gathered round call her "Jesus-Mary."

"It ain't no fun in hell, y'all," Jesus-Mary shouts. "Don't nobody want to be there. And them that does, well you sure don't want to be around *that* kind."

She's wearing an ankle-length dashiki dress, mostly yellow with a crazy crisscross of random black-green-red stripes and polygons. Her makeup is heavy on eyeliner and red-orange lipstick.

"Ever body here, ever body who can hear ole Mary's voice, you already got a vacation ticket and you don't even knows it."

Some people listen and nod, bowing heads when Jesus-Mary leads a prayer or reads one of her favorite verses. A few raise their hands to the sky.

"You can vacation forever, sitting right there next to our beloved Savior. Sitting right there in a big ole La-Z-Boy, basking in eternal love. Eternal forgiveness. Might be sippin' a lemonade. Maybe ice tea. The Good Lord is a won'erful host."

Many grin or chuckle in nervousness, not knowing what else to do. Cover their mouths and shake their heads, with that telling expression on their faces: *Why do I feel uncomfortable and embarrassed? I'm not the one creating a spectacle. Is she a trans? Yeah, that's a wig.*

A school bus arrives to shuttle grade schoolers back to the suburbs from their field trip to the city's main library. Their teacher—a short, chubby woman wearing a skirt and running shoes, looking all of eighteen—lines the kids up single file as they leave the library and marches them to the bus. "Third Grade," she calls to them, "manners!"

The kids walk right by me, each looking me over as they trip past, brilliant sponges absorbing the world, buzzing with life. But I don't see a line of random kids; I see two dozen saucer-eyed Joeys. The Joeys of a lost future.

My throat knots. I can barely swallow. A compulsion pushes me almost to the point of reaching out to let each head pass beneath my outstretched fingers, like a farmer in his wheat. I want one of them to grab my hand and say, "Where have you been? Let's go home."

"Babies, babies," Jesus-Mary says to the children. "The Good Lord keeps you from all harm. He watching over your life."

Keeps you from harm? Tell that to Joey! Her cartoonish proselytizing knocks something loose in me. Deep in my chest, a chain flies off its sprocket.

"Horse shit!" I bark at her. *Did I say that out loud?*

Jesus-Mary freezes and holds me in a long stare. There's an almost audible group inhale among the bystanders. Flashing Hollywood teeth, she cries out, "God is love!"

"Crap," I say, but not so loud this time.

The young teacher hurries the last of her class onto the bus, her face ashen with fright.

"Ain't no way but through Christ!"

"Garbage!"

"For God so loved the world . . ."

"Horse shit!"

A bicycle cop arrives on the corner across the street from us, talking into her shoulder radio.

"Show's over," the cop shouts, miming a parting motion with her hands, like a referee separating boxers. I skulk away toward the library entrance.

"Don't pay him no mind," Jesus-Mary tells the crowd as I disappear through the revolving door. "He don't mean nothin.'"

*   *   *

One escape strategy I try with Ducky is just blowing past her in the morning.

"Gotta run. Gonna miss the bus. Bye!"

"Wait! How about ordering Thai tonight? Sound good, sweetheart?"

"I may be late. Working on a major project for . . . Procter & Gamble. Can't miss my bus."

"Are you ever getting your car back from the shop? What in God's name are they doing? It's been weeks now."

"The transmission needs re-flubberizing, or they have to rebuild the flux capacitor or something. It's a major repair for sure. They're having a hard time getting all the parts."

"For a *Ford*? Ridiculous! You want me to call them for you? I'll threaten to rake them over the coals on Facebook."

"Thanks, but no. I'll call them from work." I get one leg out the door, but she ropes me right back in.

"Oh, don't take that damn bus. Baby, you can drive my car."

I look at her for a beat or two, then burst into laughter, laughing so hard I have to lean against the door frame.

"Good one. Really," I say, drying one eye with my fancy Dead Rob shirt-sleeve. She blinks at me in puzzlement, straight-faced. A flash of insult ruffles her brow and mouth.

"No, I mean it. You're welcome to borrow my car any time."

I stifle the laughing but can't corral the gone-cuckoo grin she must be seeing.

"What's wrong with my car? It's not *that* old. Could use a washing, sure."

Ducky didn't hear it. She doesn't get it at all. The Beatles reference in what she said: *Baby you can drive my car*.

Mariela adored the Beatles. Worshipped them, actually, which I always thought strange since we were born twenty-five years after they split. Could play almost every song on guitar or piano. Kept a library of books about every aspect of their career. She taught music at Estabrook Junior High in the Greenhaven suburb of Cincinnati—where we lived before Kroger—and never failed to weave Beatles songs into her lesson plans.

She and Dad bonded instantly over music, especially the Beatles. He grew up with them, buying every album and learning every chord. When I brought her home to Oklahoma to meet my parents the first time— we were both freshmen at Xavier University in Cincinnati—Mom and I were left at the firepit while Dad and Mariela rocked out one Lennon and McCartney song after another in the garage, Mariela on lead and Dad on bass.

Dad gave Mariela an expensive twelve-string acoustic on her twenty-third birthday, and she could stop your heart when she played that thing and sang "Imagine." We'd drop in on open mic nights at pubs and bars all around the Cincinnati area where she'd bring the rowdiest crowd to silence in five chords. Almost to reverence. Yeah, that was the sweetest of the sweet.

*   *   *

Some days I don't take a direct route from downtown to Ducky's house, but jump a northbound bus to Kramer & Wilson Pawn in Blue Ash. There are pawn shops on my usual eastern route to Greenhaven, but I have a special attachment to K&W.

Today I'm in a window seat, head leaning against the glass. The bus is just beginning its slow roll into traffic when Jesus-Mary walks by, pulling a garden wagon loaded with homemade Jesus swag: stacks of handwritten flyers, bad photocopies of Christ ascending to heaven, a couple dozen brightly colored pocket-sized Bibles.

She looks up from the sidewalk, and our gazes lock for a moment. She smiles at me, sparing not a single one of those sparkling teeth. I shoot her the finger. She blows me a kiss.

I take the bus out of my way to K&W Pawn to sell Morgan silver dollars my grandmother gave me before she died. I sell just a few at a time so I have an excuse to keep coming back. To keep making this detour north so I can stare at Mariela's twelve-string.

I stand and stare at it like a gravestone. Mariela doesn't have a marker anywhere because her parents spread her ashes on a beach in Mexico, not far from the village where she grew up. I come here as often as I can because one day I'll walk in and it'll be gone, dissolved back into the world like the ashes on that beach.

But it's here today, still on display behind the counter, propped between an R2-D2 ice chest and a bronze flying pig statuette. I stare. And listen.

Sometimes I can almost hear it.

*   *   *

Ducky catches me coming in from downtown and insists on dinner. Or if not dinner, then at least drinks. She has ginever of course, and I sip a Diet Coke and try to position myself where I can't see any of the always-on TVs in the house, because the second anniversary of Kroger is soon and you never know what video the cable pigs will run next.

"You don't drink at all, honey?"

"Not really, no."

"Is it a religious thing?"

"It just doesn't work for me anymore," I say.

Unless you count my vow to suffer for Mariela and Joey as a religion. To abstain from all salve or respite because I breathe and they don't. Then yeah, maybe it is a religious thing.

Ducky drinks and talks and drinks and yaks nonstop, telling me things I can't unhear. Communiqués from her Facebook posse. Things she's seen on YouTube or the History Channel. She tells me about a secret alien spaceport beneath the Pentagon. How spinach juice can cure colon cancer. That Neil Armstrong and Buzz Aldrin *did* land on the moon—that part is true, she says—but the hoax is, it wasn't *really* Armstrong and Aldrin, but Russian agents who'd had plastic surgery to look exactly like them. Apparently, Neil and Buzz were held for decades in a Siberian gulag where they died. I didn't know that. She's full of this stuff.

Without warning, she pauses a long while and inspects the ice in her glass, as if to decipher some meaning. Could be my chance to leave, so I stand.

"Rob had a second family," she says. "In Saint Louis. I didn't know until a couple of years after he passed. A wife and twin boys. They're about your age now." She sips her drink detachedly, her face as still as if she's announced the grass needs mowing.

"Oh shit," is all I can come up with as I sit back down. "I'm sorry."

She sets her ginever on the copper coffee table and takes a deep breath and fights to hold herself in check.

"I try not to think about it. Them. The others," she says at last. "After this much time, I do an OK job of it."

There's no evidence in the house of rage or vindictiveness. A portrait of Dead Rob and Ducky with their two daughters hangs over the fireplace. The girls are teens in the picture. They're my age now.

"What else *can* you do?" I say, but each thing I say seems more stupid than the last. I don't have any experience with such conversations, the awkwardness.

"But I'll confess," she says. "There's one question I want answered. Well, I *think* I want the answer. One of those *'be careful what you ask for'* things."

I look away, at the fake flowers in the fireplace, away from her pain.

We've never talked about Kroger. And I'm not ready to trade confessions. "What I want to know—what I *need* to know—were me and the girls number one? Or were we number two?"

* * *

Ducky comes to the attic with two ginevers. They're both for her. She comes up here in the night to the place Dead Rob built—where his clothes live now. Where she can smell him.

Unlike our foodless breakfasts and sundown cocktails, there's no talking. She drops her kimono and gets in my bed, some parts of her warm and some cold. There's muscle memory of skin-on-skin, hands sliding along. A curve of neck, the small of the back. An echo of old songs and lost causes. She comes to the top of her house in the night, and we align our wounds.

I can't share Kroger. That would be too intimate. But I can lie here with her, briefly dodging the loneliness, dark on dark.

Ducky snores for an hour before she startles awake and silently shuffles down the stairs as fast as plantar fasciitis will allow. In lieu of sleep, I stand by the window where moonlight splinters through the blinds and tattoos my bare chest with bright angled stripes.

Ducky says researchers in Norway have proven lack of sleep kills you. I sure hope so.

* * *

Today's Saturday and Ducky thinks I'm in the office grinding out overtime code on my fictitious P&G project. Instead, I'm downtown, sitting in Fountain Square, watching a peregrine falcon hunt for pigeons in the glass and concrete canyons.

The raptor dives and jets around a corner out of sight. I take a sip of coffee and spot a young woman with long black hair across the square—walking away from me, carrying a baby in one of those backpack papoose things.

Her size, the tilt of her head, the hair and hips and gait, from behind at least, is the twin of Mariela. I'm instantly enthralled, can't take my eyes off her. And the baby is a little melon-headed beauty, a gem plucked straight from some trove of crown jewels. I have to see her face and get a closer look at the baby. I follow them. Stalk them really, feeling like a perv, hoping I'm hanging back far enough that she doesn't notice.

One block. Two blocks. Onward. There were other people headed this way, providing cover, but now everyone has broken off, and it's just the Mariela twin out ahead and me a half block back. I should stop, turn into a store or café, just stop! But I can't; their gravity is too strong. They're the sun and I'm a lost meteor, sucked right in. We round a corner and now I see her destination: Jefferson Park.

The first Saturday of each month is Flea & Fun Day at Jefferson Park, and the place becomes a cross between a disheveled Civil War camp and a busker's fair, with dozens of dingy vendors' tents, propaganda kiosks, and food trucks. People mill in all directions, slurping lemonade and wielding foot-long corn dogs like greasy lightsabers. They browse handmade jewelry and bad art and meticulously inspect weird, useless junk no one buys.

The young mother I'm stalking dives into the festive swirl of the park. She's on her phone. This is great. With a crowd of people around, I can close in without suspicion. I make my move. Just a couple of feet away now, the baby smiling at me, flapping its arms, melting my insides. She turns her face a half turn, and I can see it's not Mariela. Of course. I know it's not. Of course I know.

She's here to meet her husband. Boyfriend. Somebody. There's a quick but tender kiss. I'm almost close enough to hear the smooch noise. He's a damn good-looking guy with shiny brown curls leaking out of a Cincinnati Bengals cap. I hate his guts. Their baby reaches a fat little hand toward me, and I have to turn away before I break down sobbing like a sad clown, ruining everyone's circus.

Jesus-Mary's clarion voice rings out from the festival's "no vendor" zone in front of the bandstand. She's set her show up on the steps of the bandstand and is earnestly hollering Bible messages. A mixed crowd is gathering: long-term neighborhood residents beside their hipster gentrifiers, and a sprinkling of suburbanites who drive in to Flea & Fun Day each month to gawk.

"Jesus Christ loves ever human on Earth," Jesus-Mary raises a giant red heart she's rough-cut from poster board, lifting it over her head and moving it in a grand sweep from left to right in front of the crowd.

"Accept His love and live forever. Jesus loves you. Jesus protects you from evil. Though I walk through the valley of death . . ."

Bengals Man takes the baby out of its papoose holder, almost brushing the child against me. He lifts it high overhead, and the baby squeals and flails. Then he cradles that gorgeous little coconut head to his chin. Mom snaps a picture.

See that? God? That's all we wanted. Just that, no more. Was that too fucking much to ask?

The knot in my throat is back. But this time I know what it is. It's rage. Blazing, incandescent rage.

Jesus-Mary spots me knocking my way through the crowd toward her.

She lowers the big cardboard heart and points at me and sings out, "Oh, I sees you, Horsey. Welcome back!"

I make my way to the front, turn to face the crowd, and form a megaphone with my hands. I scream, "Horse shit!"

"The Good Lord loves *you*, Horsey!"

"When I say *Horse!* . . . You say *Shit!*" I stretch my arms toward the crowd on the *horse*, cheerleader style, and raise them high on the word *shit*. I get one or two callbacks on the first try. A few more on the second. Quite a few on the third. Good—it's building.

"Horse!" I call. "Shit!" shouts my chorus. Got a dozen people with me now. They're loud. Most of the others move back a step or two, either confused or appalled.

"Hey! Hey! I've seen that guy!" A hulk of a man in a black wife-beater and Harley boots is pointing at me. He's bald on top except for a buzz cut of thick red hair around the sides.

"I seen you on Facebook. Yeah. It's you, ain't it?" Red says. "That dude from the Kroger shooting? I seen you in that video, man!"

His words knife into me.

"Hey, Kroger!" Yet another voice booms nearby. "You ain't worth a *fuck!*"

Needles surge from my gut, pricking up and down my spine, and my head loses all heft, ready to float off.

"You are forgiven, Horsey! Anything!" Jesus-Mary shouts.

"Horse," I cry out to my faction. My voice fractures this time. Only a muted, half-hearted "Shit" comes back to me.

"Hor . . ." I begin again. The next *horse* is halfway out my mouth when something hard and swift thwacks the back of my skull.

I bend forward, covering my head. Stagger away from the blow. There's blood on my hand, and seeing the blood woozies me out, so I drop to one knee and watch a blurred zoetrope of action: an old woman in

DayGlo Crocs and a Reds T-shirt standing over me, cane raised for an-other strike. "Heathen!" she cries. People scattering in a flurry of legs and flying corn dogs. A homeless man with greasy Einstein hair tackling the old woman to the ground.

A police cruiser sounds a woop-woop, and the sweet, lush tone of Mariela's twelve-string fills my ears and I hear her singing "Imagine" and *oh, Mariela, you know I'm not strong. I proved it. I'm not strong enough to imagine there's no heaven. Because without heaven, you and Joey have no-where to go. And without hell, I have nowhere to be.*

I blink through damp eyes and see nothing but a spiral of chaos and the red-blue strobe of the cruiser. That, and Jesus-Mary pulling me to my feet. She loosens a bright scarf from her neck and presses it to my bleeding head, then guides me toward the steps of the bandstand.

"C'mon, Horsey," she says. "I gotcha."

Bonfire

DADDY AND I always ride our horses on Thanksgiving morning, but today is more special than usual. He has something important he wants to show me. "Don't tell anyone," he says.

This is our tradition, since I was five. Daddy's sixty now and I'm sixteen. My older brother James doesn't go because he's afraid of horses, which is quite a problem when you're one of the heirs to a quarter horse breeding business. My younger sister Zelda doesn't go either. She'd rather work in the kitchen with my mother and grandmother and aunts, chopping and mixing and baking like fiends for Thanksgiving dinner later in the day.

As we head out, Nana scolds me, "Lizzy, riding a horse won't teach you cooking!" I just smile and keep pulling on my boots, too smart to take her bait. Daddy comes to my defense: "Horses are a lot more fun than dead turkeys, aren't they, darling?"

We're saddled up and on the trail by eight, planning to do the full twelve-mile perimeter of our acreage. These are my favorite hours of the year, one of the few times it's just the two of us. I'm so proud to ride with him, to have him teach me about our place. Where the quail run. Where to dig for arrowheads. The best spots for turkey and deer in the fall. And wildflowers in the spring.

Daddy has a thermos of hot chocolate and shortbread cookies, and we stop at the halfway point of our ride in a marshy area near the Red River, which marks our land's northern border with the Hightower ranch. We pause and look across the water from Texas into Oklahoma.

Here, there's a wide stand of river birch mixed with towering cotton-
woods and scrub cedars. We tie up the horses and walk a few feet into
the trees and sit on a log. Daddy pours chocolate into tin cups that warm
our hands, and we munch the cookies, sip our drinks, and watch the fog
swirl and drift along the river.

After a while Daddy says, "Keep your seat." He goes over to Zeus, his
big Appaloosa, and pulls a bouquet of supermarket flowers from his
saddlebag, a mix of daisies and mums and greenery. He walks back my
way and I brighten, thinking the flowers are for me, but he passes right
by me and says, "Come with me." I set my cup on a rock and follow him
about a hundred yards up a short rise into a clearing in the woods, not
far from the river bank.

Daddy looks back and forth a minute, getting his bearings. He points at a
particularly large birch on the edge of the clearing. We walk to it, and he
takes off his gloves and runs his fingers along a scabbed-over gash in the
trunk, shaped like a diamond. He touches it lightly, almost caressing it.

Daddy lines himself up with the scar, steps away from the tree, and
counts aloud fifteen paces. He removes the pink tissue paper and cello-
phane from the flowers and places them carefully on the ground at our
feet. We stand still in the cold and quiet of the trees, wind knocking the
high leafless branches all around, and stare silently at the flowers for a
long moment. They're the only speck of color on a great moldering floor
of drab leaves and soggy rot. Why here, I wonder? A relative we never
talk about?

"Lizzy, it's clear to me now that you'll wind up running this ranch when
I'm gone. James don't want nothing to do with it, and frankly, I don't think
Zelda's smart enough." I look down at the flowers as he speaks, blushing
and mute, not knowing where else to look or what to say.

"I'm going to tell you something nobody else knows," he says. "This is something you need to know to be a good steward of our land. Our land is everything. Our land is legacy."

His voice has an edge of pain to it, and he scans about a thousand yards upriver as he speaks.

"Your great-great-granddaddy Avery Bingham once found a squatter living in these woods. Right here in this clearing. None of them knew how he got here. Could've floated in on a handmade raft or something.

"This squatter built himself a little cabin out of deadfall, tied together with baling twine. Had a cedar branch roof and a rock firepit. It was right about in here." He waves his hand around, pointing at no particular place.

"Ole Avery came down here and told him to clear out. The vagrant refused. Avery came down several days running and tried to reason with him, but the man just wouldn't leave. Finally, Avery went to the sheriff, but the sheriff told him: 'I don't have time to ride out to your place every time a hobo shows up. Just run him off best you can.'

"So, Avery and his son Seth—my granddaddy Seth—came down here to try again. They argued with the man quite awhile, and at one point the man wrapped himself around a tree and they had to pry him off. After they dragged him off the tree, he sat by his firepit and cried and threw tin cans at them. He finally got up and Avery and Seth thought it was over, but he took a swing at Seth and the two of them got into a fistfight. They rolled in the dirt and through the firepit. Seth said it was a hard fight. The vagrant was small and scrawny and much stronger than he looked, but Seth was younger and got the better of him. Seth held him down until Avery said, 'Let him up.' When the squatter got on his feet, Avery said, 'So you ain't leaving?'

'I ain't leaving,' the man said.

That's when Avery shot him dead."

I look at Daddy, and he looks me in the face for the first time in the telling of this secret. He's as sad as a pallbearer, and I want to cry—partly because of the story and partly because it pains me that I have no words to soothe my father.

"What did the sheriff have to say about that?" I ask.

"Nothing. They never told the sheriff or anybody about it. They went home and came back with a wagon load of pine boards, built a coffin, and buried the poor bastard right here, where I just put these flowers."

"They killed a man and buried him in the woods? Like a . . . dog? Jesus."

"Honey, things were different back then. People had to handle things on their own. I'm not saying it was *right*, just that it was *necessary*. It's like Granddaddy Seth used to say: 'If you don't control the ground where you walk, somebody else will. Which way you want it?'"

I stare at the flowers so small and lost in the sweep of the clearing, like a whispered prayer in an abandoned church.

"Somewhere along the way, Seth started bringing flowers down here every year about this time, then he passed that job to my dad, who gave it to me. Lizzy, I'd like you to keep it up after I go, if you're willing."

I nod and ask, "What was his name?"

"Don't know, baby. No one ever knew."

My horse Doc snorts and shakes his head. We take this as a signal, walk out of the woods and mount up. As we ride away, Daddy motions east and west with his arms and says, "Come spring, I'm building a fence across this line and cutting these woods off. I don't want anybody wandering around down here."

*   *   *

We eat our Thanksgiving feast around three o'clock. It's always a crowd, lots of aunts and uncles along with a dozen cousins—some of them grown, some of them kids.

After the meal, the women gather around the great room fireplace and shoo out all the children and men so Nana can bring out her secret stash of Pappy Van Winkle bourbon. She thinks it's secret, but everyone knows where she hides it, although no one knows where she gets it.

I'm still too young to be allowed in on the fun, so I go out where the kids are playing and the men are finishing up the woodpile for the annual Bingham family bonfire. They're building it twenty feet high. They say it can be seen for miles across the open pastures in every direction, even all the way to the interstate.

After dark, the women bundle up and walk down behind the main stables to the bonfire site. Soon after, families from neighboring ranches start arriving, and one of my uncles swings a flashlight and manages the parking. Daddy brews cowboy coffee for the adults and hot chocolate for the kids on a Coleman stove set up near the woodpile. Then he climbs up in a pickup bed, puts two fingers to his mouth, and whistles everybody to attention.

"Thank y'all for coming. I've got an announcement. I'm not going to tell the story this year . . ."

The crowd gives a moan of disappointment, thinking they're not going to hear the story.

"Lizzy's going to tell the story tonight. Lizzy, get on up here."

I'm shocked and scared. I've never spoken to a crowd this large. The story is very important to my family. The story *is* my family. I know it by heart, but I've never told it at the bonfire before. I climb up in the truck bed, and Daddy sees I'm shaking a little so he winks and rubs my shoulder, and that calms me down.

"On this site," I begin, and point to the enormous pile of logs and kindling soaked in diesel, "our ancestor Jonah Bingham built a cabin for his family. Jonah and Lilith Bingham lived here with their three children, Avery, Hope, and Katherine. In late November, 1873, they were attacked in one of the last Comanche raids in North Texas. Jonah was butchering a hog when he spotted about twenty warriors bearing down on him on horseback, led by a war chief known as Red Knife." Daddy signals me to speak up.

"Jonah was wounded near the smokehouse but made it to the cabin where Lilith and the girls were hiding. Avery was gone, having left home the day before, riding with two Texas Rangers to Fort Worth so he could apprentice with a lawyer. Jonah and Lilith fought the raiders from their cabin until she was fatally wounded."

This is where I have to be careful what I say.

"By sunset, both girls were dead, and the cabin was on fire."

Here's the part we never tell: Jonah killed his daughters to keep them from being taken by the Comanches, then set fire to the cabin.

"Jonah climbed on the roof and battled the warriors while his home burned beneath his feet. Out of ammunition, he was shot from the rooftop. Mortally wounded but still alive, Jonah slashed Red Knife's face with a razor as the chief bent over to see if he was finally dead.

"Red Knife was impressed. He slit Jonah's throat and forbade any of his men to take the scalp. The chief declared this place—this place we now call home—to be honored ground, and ordered that anyone who shows disrespect from here to each horizon be burned alive.

"The warriors wrapped Jonah in a blanket and buried his body over there," I pause and point to a towering post oak a few yards from the bonfire site, not far from the main house, "near that big tree." Daddy shines a flashlight on a cluster of gravestones under the tree where I'm pointing.

"Avery returned from Fort Worth and buried what remains he could find of his mother and sisters, all of them near that tree. Fifty years later he was placed there too.

"Red Knife was eventually captured by Texas Rangers, and before they hanged him, he gave an account of the battle and of Jonah Bingham's courage. The story I tell you tonight is the true story of our family."

Other than a muffled cough or two, the crowd is still and quiet.

"Every Thanksgiving, the Binghams build a bonfire on this site in thanks for our survival and in memory of all in our family who have passed over the years. May God rest their souls."

I signal Uncle Clark to light the fire, then jump down from the truck to applause and backslaps.

Daddy gives me a bear hug and kisses the top of my head. "Good job, sweetie." I hug him back, pleased that he's pleased, but mostly relieved to have it over.

As the fire grows bigger and hotter, the crowd's mood swings from somber to celebratory. Beer comes out of coolers. People chatter about football and weather and politics. Nana circles around the flames—cane in one hand, an old fashioned in the other. She shouts out to my mother, "Don't you even *think* about burying me under that damn tree!"

I walk away from everybody, down past the stables, the fire so strong it reaches me even this far, warming my back as a cold gust chaps my face. Daddy comes up behind me and hands me a mug of coffee. He puts a splash of Pappy in it.

"You know I'm not allowed."

"You are tonight."

He walks away and leaves me to my thoughts. I admire the stars awhile before looking down into the darkness, toward the river. I sip the coffee and cringe at its bitterness and picture a nameless vagrant, sitting on a stump outside his tumbledown hut. He didn't get a fire. He didn't get a gravestone.

And I'm sure he disagrees with Red Knife about this being honored ground.

Pocketknife

KEVIN HAD NEVER seen his father cry. A man didn't cry. But if he did, he didn't do it in front of his twelve-year-old. Not in public. Not while eating ice cream.

Only thirty minutes earlier, Kevin had been sitting in Mrs. Beeker's classroom watching her bony finger trace the route of Lewis and Clark from Saint Louis to the Pacific. Then Principal Douglas had poked his dour face into Beeker's room and pointed at him.

He'd figured he was following Principal Douglas down the hallway because of his note to Tonya Fuentes: "I don't give a shit what my mama thinks about your family, I want to be your boyfriend." Principal Douglas hadn't mentioned the note but led him to the school's office where Eddie, Kevin's father, was waiting.

They'd left the school and walked through sleet to Eddie's pickup. Kevin bowed his head against the weather and ran his fingers along the rust-bitten haunches of the old Dodge.

"Why am I leaving school early?"

"Just wanted to see my boy."

It took three cranks to start the arthritic truck before they limped off toward what was left of the dying town.

"Mama told us you ran off. Said you weren't coming back."

"She's liable to say anything about me. But you listen," Eddie had pointed a bandaged finger at the boy, "I'm not leaving my kids. Not never."

Kevin had stayed quiet for the rest of the drive to Greer's Truck Stop, not saying a word as Eddie hustled him out of the truck and into a booth near the back. Eddie had ordered strawberry ice cream for himself and chocolate for the boy, and they'd eaten in silence from frigid metal cups, glazed with ice.

Now, Kevin watched fat tears slide down his father's face. Eddie made no sound and turned his head to the wall. Then he looked at his son, forced a smile, and pulled a pocketknife from his coat, still in its box. It was the official Boy Scout four-blade pocketknife Kevin had coveted for so long, the knife Eddie had refused to buy two months before.

"Too goddamn expensive," he'd said at the time. "Damn Scouts. Good at beating a man out of his paycheck."

Kevin stared at the knife a long moment before touching it. He took off the clear cover and tilted the box so the knife slipped into his hand. He loved the heft of it. Caressed the fake wood casing. He wanted to show Eddie a happy, grateful face, but guilt dampened his smile. Guilt at having caused this extravagance.

"What're you waiting for?" Eddie said. "Let's see it already."

Kevin snagged the crescent groove of the main blade and unfolded it. The mirrored finish caught the light and threw a beam across the cafe.

"How 'bout a 'thanks' for Dad?"

He managed a faint "thank you," shamed by the thought of how many skipped lunches it must have cost.

"I don't know why you can't come back home."

"She don't want me no more. Hates me working out of town so much."

"Will y'all divorce?"

Eddie shook his head slowly and shrugged. "All I know is I love your mama." The boy was sure he'd never heard his father say the word *love* before.

"There been any strange men over to the house?" Eddie shoved tears away from both eyes with the back of a thick hand, cracked and red from too much winter. The boy looked down at the knife, afraid to be the cause of more trouble.

Should he tell him about Glenn, who drove them to Longview in his big Lincoln to eat catfish and spend the night in a place with connected rooms—a double door in between—one room for Kevin and his little sisters, and the other for Mama and Glenn?

And there was Swank, who took them to his hunting cabin. Mama had pushed him to pal around with the guy all weekend, the two of them hiking to an ancient Caddo burial mound where Swank lined up pine cones across the top of the sacred grave and let Kevin blast away at them with a pistol.

"I got to pee," he said. He didn't want to see more tears, and he didn't want to see Swank's gun anywhere near his father. He stood and closed the knife and pushed it into his jeans.

Eddie nodded. "I'll fill up the Dodge. Meet me out front."

The boy peed and as he washed his hands, he noticed the small, narrow rectangle of a window a couple of feet above the sink. It was an old casement window with a metal frame and a handle centered on the bottom edge that turned ninety degrees to lock. The glass was opaque and crisscrossed with silvery wire cables in a diamond pattern, like a strip of skin cut from a huge, translucent snake.

Standing on the sink, he pulled at the handle, but the window wouldn't budge. He opened the knife and sliced into layers of paint along one side of the frame, cutting all the way back to the Clinton administration. He worked the knife around the frame and pulled again. The window popped open with a violent wash of cold air. Kevin pocketed the knife.

It was a close fit, but he pushed his head and shoulders through the window. A short drop and he was standing among a half dozen trash barrels. He squinted into a numbing wind and looked across a double set of railroad tracks. A wide, flat pasture lay beyond the tracks, leading to a thick growth of pines.

He could make it to the woods. Before the Dodge was full and Eddie came looking for him. Before he had to choose.

Tender, Like My Heart

TEDI LOVED COLE the way girls love their first love, the way birds love sky. She met him just a few days after lung cancer killed her father. Cole swept in on her at a gas station, trailing an anarchy of long blond hair and straddling a black Harley that growled *let's fuck.* As word got around, Tedi's friends—and the Wexlers, her new foster parents—shook their heads and clicked their tongues, knowing he was the worst possible thing for her, but she was sixteen and smothering in afterdeath, and Cole was a master at cutting just the right filly from the herd.

First, he paid for her father's funeral. For weeks after that kindness, Tedi brightened just at the sight of Cole. Then he took his time and gave her the full girlfriend treatment. Dinners at Outback and Red Lobster. Earrings and bracelets shoplifted by his stoner brother Eldred. Crazed kamikaze runs with Tedi on the back of his bike, roaring across the Ohio River from where she lived in Covington, Kentucky, into Cincinnati to see a movie or get Graeter's, which Tedi knew was Oprah's favorite ice cream.

"Oprah, huh?" Cole said. "Then we're getting us some Oprah."

After a few months, he eased her into the H. It took about ten days for the junk to snake itself around her reason and convince her she needed to pull her weight—like Cole kept saying—she needed to blow truckers for money. Money to buy more Kentucky White Horse. He pimped her at truck stops up and down I-75 from Cincinnati to Knoxville. After a while Cole stopped using with her, but she didn't notice. She was loving the Horse more and Cole less.

By her nineteenth birthday, she wanted out. About sunrise, she crawled across the floor of a crash house in Covington, pawing over four of Cole's other girls, and made it out the back door into the steam cloud of an August morning. She took a thick bite of phlegmy air, picked a random direction, and started moving. Walking at first, then running.

*   *   *

Three weeks later Eldred tracked her to Dekker House, a tattered, faded Victorian mansion two blocks off the river, converted in the seventies to a women's shelter and rehab center. She was through the worst part of withdrawal, each new clean day restoring a lost piece of her. The meetings and methadone were just beginning to take hold, and she felt her head getting straight for the first time since the funeral.

Tedi peeked out a second-floor window and saw Eldred on the front steps. The premature bald spot at the crown of his head gawked up at her, like a Cyclops eye the size of her fist, surrounded by buzz cut. She knew she'd have to deal with Cole and his stoner brother sooner or later, so she came downstairs, pushed forward by the newly learned happy-talk bouncing around her skull. The happy-talk said, over and over, "You can do it! You can do it! Tell him to fuck off!" She scanned the front yard and up and down the street to make sure there were plenty of people around. She stepped out on the porch.

"Are you fucking crazy?" Eldred said, palms up, rattling his head from side to side.

"I'm out," Tedi said. "Just tell Cole I'm out."

"Girl, it don't work that way. Cole told me to drag your ass back. *Today*. Drag it hard, if needed."

Faye, the house manager, a stout, fiftyish woman with a long gray ponytail, kept passing by the door, watching them. I don't want her in my business, Tedi thought. She decided Faye couldn't hear anything.

"No more," Tedi said. Eldred glared and shook his head.

"No more tricks. No H. No Cole," she said, intending the words to be full and solid, but feeling cracks and quivers in each syllable.

Faye stepped out on the porch. "Tedi? You OK, hon?"

"Yeah. We're done." Tedi couldn't look either of them in the eye. Faye gave Eldred a disapproving huff but went back inside.

"You know we're not done," Eldred said as soon as the house manager was out of earshot. "Nothing's done till Cole says."

*　*　*

At dusk, Tedi and three housemates walked along the riverfront, talking and watching downtown Cincinnati light up in the distance. Darkness washed in under a cloudless sky, and soon everyone headed back to Dekker House except Tedi. She sat on a bench looking across the river at the Cincinnati Reds stadium. That bench had been a favorite destination for her and her father, Digger Shay, during their evening walks, especially when the Reds were in town.

She looked across the still, black sheen of the river toward the stadium, all its lights blazing for a late season game. It took a long while, but her patience was rewarded. Home run. Fireworks. Red, yellow, blue, and green slashes across the dark skin of night.

"Look," Digger used to tell her, "you get double for your money, in the sky *and* the river." She laughed at the memory, how he said the same thing every time, pointing up with one arm and down with the other as the brilliant reflections snaked out across the water toward them.

It had always been just the two of them. It wasn't that Tedi didn't remember her mother—she just considered her irrelevant. Joanne Shay vanished one autumn afternoon while six-year-old Tedi napped and Digger laid bricks on a new bank jutting up on the north edge of Covington, not far from where she now sat watching the fireworks. The police interviewed Digger several times about his wife's disappearance, because the husband is always suspect number one, but it was soon clear that Joanne had drained their small savings and made a run for it.

When Joanne left, Digger quit a good job as a bricklayer to manage a convenience store, Fast Freddie's. He never complained about it or said anything, but Tedi knew he did it so he could be around when she came home from school every day. They rented the apartment above the store. Tedi got off her school bus at the corner directly across the street, and Digger was always standing in the front door of the store, waving.

"Hey, hey Doodle-Girl. Good day?" Digger said as she made her way— through narrow aisles of overpriced tobacco, snacks, beer, and wine—to the back of the store and the staircase that led up to their small apartment.

"Good day," she said in grade school.

"OK day," she said in junior high.

"Just a day," she said in high school, as long as it lasted, until Digger got sick. Then all days turned bad.

The stadium emptied and the lights went out, but Tedi stayed on the bench and watched moonlight twist and stretch in the wakes of passing boats. A tug moved downriver, pushing five huge flats of coal, each flat half a block long. She remembered Digger talking about how dangerous the tugs were to pleasure boaters.

"After a few beers, you're not paying good attention. Let your boat drift.

At night you never see 'em coming till it's too late. Can't hear 'em neither. How can something so big and so deadly just sneak up on you like that?"

*   *   *

The doctors told them he had a significant spot on his left lung. They biopsied the spot and said that without treatment, he'd be dead in a year. But they might be able to slow it down, or maybe even stop it, with radiation and chemo. They blasted and juiced him for six weeks.

She shouldn't worry, he said. The Good Lord would take care of him. All his life, the Good Lord had always taken care of him. Tedi heard this every day. When does that start, exactly? This would be a good time for that to start.

For a while, Digger was still in the doorway of the store waving when Tedi got off the bus, but the spot grew bigger and spread its tendrils. In the last few weeks of his life, Digger was upstairs in bed when Tedi got off the bus and made her way through all the chips and alcohol and past Salvio, the man who bought the building and took over the store.

"I'm afraid your father is faring worse today, Miss Shay. His coughing is incessant. I don't want to be insensitive," Salvio lowered his voice, "but it is not good for business. Why don't you make him some tea? Maybe that will help."

*   *   *

As bad as it was during the day, Digger's coughing raged at night. Tedi couldn't sleep any at first, but as the nights passed, she lapsed into long periods of half-sleep, tuning out the sound like sad, ragged waiting-room

Muzak. She checked on him from time to time, shocked to see him asleep, or at least in an altered state. Who knew a dying man could cough in his sleep?

She slept on the floor by his bed some nights, and dreamt of the two of them, his hacking and fighting for breath a faint, macabre soundtrack to the dreams. Her mind replayed them cruising on the B&B Riverboat for her tenth birthday. Of them chicken dancing to hokey polka music at Oktoberfest. Digger surprising her with a hideous, embarrassing party dress for a junior high dance, one she hated but didn't have the heart to reject. She wore it anyway, spending most of the dance hiding in the bathroom.

But mostly, she dreamt of hunting. Digger took her squirrel hunting with him every fall, starting when she was about five. She adored it. He'd wake her long before daylight, bundle her up in a bright orange hooded camo sweatshirt and put a dozen shotgun shells in her front pouch. Then they'd drive two hours—sometimes east to Shawnee Forest, sometimes south to the Daniel Boone Forest. Besides carrying their shells, she also carried the pale, bloodstained pillowcase they used as a game bag.

She knew the rules. Sit very still on the log or stump Digger picked for her. No talking, no fidgeting. Don't turn your head to scan the treetops; just move your eyes, side to side, up and down. Digger's place was always a few yards out in front of her, leaning against a tree with his shotgun. The squirrels, she discovered, fell in slow motion, their dive into death elegant and graceful.

Digger gutted and skinned them back at the truck when the hunt was over, rolling each one in plastic wrap and dropping them in a cooler in the truck bed. As Tedi got older, she took the job of skinning and gutting, and finally, cooking the squirrels. Gutting was simple—anybody could do that—but learning to skin properly took a couple of seasons to master.

Cooking was her downfall. Squirrel stew was not too hard, but she struggled with frying them, which was Digger's favorite. Once, when she was thirteen, she put a platter on the table alongside some canned biscuits and a bowl of atrocious gravy. The squirrels were inedible, more akin to bicycle tires than meat. Digger gnawed at them as best he could.

"How are they, Daddy?"

"Oh, they're good, little Doodle Girl," he said. "Tender, like my heart."

*   *   *

Tedi sat a long time, watching Digger sleep-cough and wheeze and choke. He'd startle awake at times and give her a smile or a weak thumbs up, then lapse back into another round of unconscious hacking.

One night during a wakeful period, Digger told her to get his guns from the closet. "Don't worry; they ain't loaded." He had a .410 Stevens single-shot shotgun for squirrel hunting and a .38 caliber Smith & Wesson revolver with busted grips held to the frame with electrician's tape.

He lifted the pistol and said, "This is damn old, but it works. Got two or three boxes of ammo in the top of that closet. Belonged to your grand-daddy Archie Shay. He was a bootlegger." He picked up the edge of the bedsheet and wiped yellow spit from his mouth.

"Once I'm gone, you keep this in your room at night. Loaded."

"I don't know how to shoot that."

"You'll learn. Use both hands. Take it out in the country and practice somewhere. Maybe down by the riverbank. You need it. You're going to be a young girl alone in the world. You hear me?"

"Yes, sir."

Digger waved the pistol as best he could, but he was too weak to hold it up long and let it flop against his thigh on the bed.

"You ever find yourself up shit creek, here's your paddle."

*   *   *

Tedi put another morphine patch on Digger and took her spot on the floor. Before she fell into sleep, she heard Digger talking to her long-gone mother.

"Where'd you go?" he said to Joanne, but his words just melted into darkness. Then she heard him talking to his childhood dog, Partner.

"Come in here, Partner," he said. "It's too cold out there. Too cold."

An angry sleep swallowed her, and she saw the cold men coming. Bloated, hoary men surfacing from the river, four of them, coming for Digger. As they drew near, Partner jumped one of them, growling and ripping putrid flesh, but neither Partner nor morphine patches could hold them off. Digger set his jaw and arched his back against the cold men. They rammed their wretched hands into him, down his throat and up his ass. They clawed at his innards.

She jolted awake to someone speaking.

"Another patch," Digger said. His words ached out thin as vapor in a voice Tedi had never heard before. Tedi knew Digger loved the Good Lord, but there was no sign the Lord loved him back. Why else would He torture her daddy to death?

She patched him again and counted what was left. Two. Digger didn't need another one that night because that was the night the cold men took him.

Tedi went downstairs to the store and got a screw-top bottle of pink wine from the cold case and went to her room. She cranked up Jack White and drank two coffee mugs full of the wine, put one of Digger's patches on her shoulder, and sank into bed. Around 4 a.m., she awoke stupefied, jutted her head over the bedside and puked.

She stutter-stepped to Digger's room and smoothed his hair. She kissed him on the forehead, and through a pained smile said, "Good Lord my ass." Then she pulled the sheet over his face and eased down into the chair across from the bed and watched the ceiling oscillate down-up down-up until she fell asleep. It was well past sunrise when she awoke and called Salvio.

Tedi waited for Salvio at the foot of Digger's bed, looking out the window across the rooftops of an insurance agent and a bail bondsman and fingering the last unopened morphine patch. She decided to save it for the funeral.

*   *   *

When Tedi's time was up at Dekker House, Faye the house manager tried to get her into Section Eight housing, but there was a nine-month waiting list. Faye worked the phone for days and finally found Tedi a shared room at the Olive Mount Convent, run by the Sisters of Holy Grace. The nuns lived on the first two floors and used the twelve rooms on the top floor of their sanctuary to provide temporary shelter for battered and abused women, the theory being that only the most deranged and debauched of men would defile two floors of elderly nuns to reach his target. Theory aside, Mother Celeste leaned on the local police until they agreed to send a patrol car by every couple of hours from sundown until dawn to dissuade intruders.

Tedi found a job at Waffle World (*We Never Close*) working midnight to six, in the kitchen at first, then later as a counter waitress. And every morning she walked the eight blocks back to the convent's kitchen (usually with a grocery bag half full of waffles) where she worked through the breakfast shift, unpaid, to earn her keep.

Her low profile would have remained low if meth-head Ronald Trulee hadn't robbed Waffle World and taken hostages one Sunday morning, triggering a SWAT siege and hours of TV coverage. After a SWAT sniper put a hole through Trulee's brain about noon, Tedi and ten other employees and customers walked out the front door of the restaurant with their hands on their heads, live on all major Cincinnati TV channels.

* * *

Two nights later, Eldred burst from his truck onto the sidewalk three feet from Tedi as she walked home to the convent. She feared the brothers had seen her on the news, and here was her proof. She sucked in a hard breath and grabbed for the pepper spray hanging from her purse strap, but Eldred was too quick and had her in a tight hug and his knife to her throat before she could spray.

"You know what I'm like, Tedi. I'll cut you if I have to." Tedi nodded. She knew it was true.

"Get in the truck." Tedi climbed in. Eldred stood on the curb and leaned against her. She felt the point of a six-inch hunting knife just below her rib cage.

"We're just going to talk," Eldred said. Tedi thought the less she said to the stooge the better, so she gave Eldred a slow nod to keep him calm while she scanned the street for anything or any idea that might save her.

"You say you want out? It ain't that easy. You owe Cole."

Tedi crinkled her brow and shifted her tongue but didn't speak. She stopped nodding.

"Oh yeah. Cole says you owe him for the funeral. Six grand. And room and board for over two years. He'll give you a discount on the living cost, 'cause you were his favorite piece. So, twenty thou total."

"Like fuck," Tedi said, unable to hold it any longer. "I don't have a dime. Besides, I made him shitloads of cash."

Eldred laid the blade flat against her cheek, just above the jaw. She sensed the cutting edge, poised to bite, but he had tilted it just enough to avoid drawing blood.

"Cole's being generous. Not charging you for all the dope you burned through."

Tedi hated it, but tears came, silent drops washing over the black steel weapon. He pointed it at her gut.

"He wants me to work it off?" Tedi asked. "Back on the road?" Tedi saw a car headed for them, hoping someone in it would see them—maybe spook Eldred away—but it turned two blocks short.

"Work it off, yeah," Eldred said. "But not on the road."

"What then?"

"You know Mama Queen?"

"I've heard the name." Some of Cole's girls talked about Mama Queen who ran a couple dozen girls in rural Clermont County, upriver from Cole's territory and across the water in Ohio.

"Cole needs her gone. You take her out, and you're free and clear."

"You mean *kill* her? Holy shit!"

"It's an easy job. She's old. Sick too, we hear."

"I'm not killing anybody. Especially not an old lady."

"Look, Cole gave Old Queenie a chance, more than one. But she won't sell. So now, well, business got to be done."

Tedi covered her face. Not enough money to run and nowhere to hide. She had been foolish to think she really could escape. She'd seen other girls try; almost all of them ended up back on the road with Cole. She tried not to think about what happened to the others, the ones Eldred didn't bring back. She lowered her hands and found the courage to look him in the eye.

"Why me? Killing people's *your* job, right?"

"You heard fight fire with fire? We figured fight whore with whore," Eldred said, pulling the knife away an inch or two. "Queen goes down, me and Cole are the first ones they'll come looking for. We plan to be drinking downtown when it happens."

She knew she was trapped. But she also knew two other things: there was no way she was turning back the clock and working truck stops for Cole again. And there was no way she was letting these assholes kill her.

"Way I see it Tedi, you got three choices," Eldred said. "Do this job for us, go back on the tail-trail, or . . ." Eldred jerked his knife back to her throat, and this time pressed it hard enough to draw a thin smear of blood at her jawbone, "I'll go ahead and use this thing."

There was no doubt Eldred meant what he said. He would kill her. Not then and there, maybe, but sometime somewhere. He might even be hoping she'd refuse. So: go after Mama Queen, another whore-runner like Cole, or go under Eldred's knife. What's one less whore-runner?

"OK, OK." She heard the words leave her mouth but couldn't believe she was saying them.

"I'll do Mama Queen. Where is she?"

Eldred cut the pepper spray loose from her purse and threw it across the street. He chunked her purse onto the sidewalk, reached into his back pocket, and handed her a bar napkin where he'd written: *3021 Rollins Creek Road, New Richmond, OH.*

"Twenty miles east of Cincinnati," Eldred said. "Take Highway 52."

* * *

Nine the next morning, she took the bus to the far south side of Covington and rang the doorbell at the Wexlers' house. After Digger died, she'd moved in as one of their foster kids and lived there almost five months until she ran off with Cole, sleeping in their basement dormitory in a long row of twin beds, one of six lost kids, age eight to seventeen.

"Mrs. Wexler?" Tedi said. "Remember me?"

"Teri?" Mrs. Wexler opened the door maybe four inches.

"Tedi."

"Oh, right. Sorry. What are you doing here?"

"Do you still have Daddy's truck?"

It felt good to be in Digger's truck again. She drove to New Richmond and followed Eldred's directions to Rollins Creek Road, a two-lane backcountry road tunneling through curtains of runaway honeysuckle, sugar maple, and red oak on the high ground, and pale-barked river birch in the bottomlands. Houses were modest and scarce, at least the houses she could see from the road. Mostly old farmhouses, built from fieldstone and plank, now finding themselves tumbledown lot-mates to trailers.

The house at 3021 looked at least eighty years old, a two-story white plank in bad need of paint, perched atop a limestone block foundation with narrow-slit basement windows. A defunct farmstead, corn and soybeans now a distant memory, woods slowly reclaiming the land.

The corpse of a metal barn stood behind the house, back where the main body of the woods began, only a dozen corroded sheets of tin left clinging to a pipe skeleton. Tedi did a drive-by in daylight to verify the address and get her bearings.

*   *   *

She came back to the house at 2 a.m. and turned off the headlights, killed the engine, and coasted down the long gravel driveway as far as inertia would carry her toward the ruined barn. There was only one car about, a nineties model Buick sedan. She sat awhile in the dark wondering if Mama Queen had bodyguards. No matter, really. No choices anymore.

There was no light in the house other than something low and dim in what was probably the kitchen, and since the Buick was dewed over, she figured it had been parked there for hours. She stuck a stubby LED flashlight into her jeans and double-checked her granddaddy's bootlegging revolver. It was fully loaded. She gathered up her supplies: a bath towel, hammer, and duct tape.

Tedi eyed a basement window at the back of the house. A tight fit maybe, but she thought her hips and shoulders would pass through. She taped the window and doubled, then tripled the large towel, pressed it against the glass, and hit it once with the hammer. Satisfied with the muted sound of the breakage, she pounded three more times until the glass hung from its frame in shards. It took awhile to peel off the tape and glass, a piece or two getting away from her and falling inside, making only a soft thud on the dirt floor.

She picked her way through the black grave of the basement—one stepping stone of LED light at a time—to the stairs leading up into the house. She tried the doorknob. No lock. Tedi eased the door open into the kitchen, took two steps, and stopped dead. She heard a grunt. The grunt turned into a low growl. She pointed her light at the growl and saw a pale little dog in its night crate. The dog growled louder, building to a full bark. Tedi knelt next to the cage, whispering.

"Hello, baby. It's OK." The dog lowered its growl and sniffed the air.

"What's your name, little guy? Little girl?" Tedi looked around for the fridge while trying to sweet-talk the dog. The dog barked once, shrill and sharp, shooting sparks through Tedi's spine, then it whined and resumed a low growl. Tedi spotted the fridge and opened it, grasping for any reasonable thing she could give the dog. Pickle loaf. She ripped out some slices, knelt and cooed.

"Here, sweetie. Look what I got." Tedi stuffed a hunk of pickle loaf through the bars into the dog's little jail. It sniffed the lunch meat then hogged it down and whined for more. Tedi fed it the last slice.

She was a compact and raggedy dog of uncertain mutthood, weighing maybe fifteen pounds after a big meal, draped in wavy fur, ashen in color except for piss-yellow smudges under each eye. The dog relished the last slice of meat and quieted, turning as best she could in the small crate, and snuggled down in her blanket—not to sleep, but positioned on her belly to watch Tedi with approving curiosity.

"That's right, doggy. Go night-night."

Tedi soft-shoed into the front parlor, turned off her LED, and stood motionless, listening. The dog was quiet, but a muted sound came from the back of the house, a swooshing. An inkling of moonlight broke through the clouds enough that she could make out a hallway that led toward the swooshing, so she guided herself blind down the hall, sliding one hand along the wallpaper, taking chopped steps.

The aged floor creaked with almost every step, and each creak raced her heart. She reached a doorway with no door on the hinges, paused, and pulled the gun from her waist, gripping it with both hands like Digger said. A nightlight in the room threw an amber halo about ankle high. Tedi crouched—she didn't know why, she'd seen it on TV—and followed her gun into the room.

Yeah, there you are, old whore-runner. The woman jerked and writhed in her sleep, propped up on three pillows. The swooshing machine—what she'd heard called a concentrator, about two feet tall—sat on the floor next to the bed. A noose of clear plastic tubing ran up from it and looped around, shooting oxygen up the woman's nose.

Tedi stepped within a foot of the old woman's head and pointed the revolver. *God, she looks old. Older than you'd think. Guess the sickness adds ten years or more. Can't breathe without that gadget. So frail. Frail as Daddy at the end. This is fucking horrible, like shooting Daddy with his own goddamn gun. Don't think,* she told herself, *just shoot.*

The machine puffed and hummed, and the old woman jerked her head to one side, crying out in her sleep. Startled, Tedi screeched, stumbled, and dropped the gun. It fired and the bullet pierced the concentrator with a flash of sparks. The contraption chugged, quit running, and the room fell quiet. Tedi dropped to the floor and groped in the darkness for the gun. *Where is the damn thing?*

"Ohhhhhh," the woman moaned as she awoke. Tedi looked up through a gauze of moonlight at the old woman, the woman's face a mix of confusion and fright. "Who?" the woman said as she struggled to drag a veiny leg out of bed. She carefully dropped one foot to the floor, then the other. Stood and swayed for a moment, gasping for air.

She took one step and groaned before her knees buckled. Her head slammed the nightstand with an audible *thwack* as she fell, scattering pill bottles like bowling pins. The woman landed face down, barely three feet from where Tedi crouched. Motionless. Silent.

Tedi stood. She reached out with her foot and tapped the woman's shin. No movement. She got a little braver and toed the woman's butt. She pressed her foot against the woman's pelvis and rocked. Again, with her foot, Tedi rolled the woman over on her back and crouched beside her. She wasn't breathing. Nasty gash on her forehead. A crown of blood. Tedi felt for a pulse on the wrist and then again on the neck. No pulse, no breathing. Time to get out.

She found the pistol and made her way back to the kitchen where the little dog leapt to her feet, hopeful. She glanced at the dog, hesitated a moment, but kept moving. Tedi gathered the hammer, tape, and towel and drove away. Leaving the dog locked in that cage, alone, weighed on her, but she figured Mama Queen's own version of Eldred would show up there tomorrow. He'd see to the dog.

*   *   *

The next night, Tedi came out a side door of the convent already late for her shift at Waffle World and saw Eldred sitting in his truck across the parking lot. He waved her over. What now?

There was no real path of escape, other than to cower back into the building where she'd have to make a last-minute call to work with some excuse. Can't risk losing that job. She walked to Eldred's truck.

"Get in," Eldred said. "I'll give you a lift."

"That's OK. I'll take mine." She pointed at Digger's battered little pickup. Eldred put his Ford in reverse and backed up four spaces, hemming her vehicle between two cars.

"Get in this goddamn truck, Tedi. We gotta talk. I'm already pissed— don't make it worse."

Tedi got in, and Eldred drove four blocks to Founders Park and pulled off next to a duck pond.

"You know where Mama Queen was today?" Eldred barked at her. "Riding her fat ass through Sam's Club on that old-fart scooter of hers."

"No way!" Tedi said. "She's dead!"

"Cole seen her there himself."

"Eldred, please, I was in her house, standing over her body. Maybe Cole saw somebody else?"

"You think he's stupid?" Eldred slapped the steering wheel with both hands.

"I'm not lying. Eldred, please! I did what you wanted. I took care of it. She was *dead* when I left there."

"OK then. How'd you do it?"

"I, uh, smothered her."

"*Smothered?* Shit. How do you know she didn't just pass out and then wake up later? Smothered for fuck's sake. When did this vicious smothering take place?"

"Last night. I drove out there, parked up close to the old barn, then broke in through a basement window."

"*Old barn?* There's no old barn." Eldred squinted at Tedi. "And the house doesn't have a basement." She struggled to make sense of what he was saying. What's going on here? Is this some kind of scam?

"The barn in back of the house! Near the woods!" Tedi pleaded, confused, looking for some glint of confirmation from Eldred.

"You talking about a red brick ranch? Three-car garage?" he said. A cold wave hit Tedi. Her mind raced. What is he talking about? That's not the place at all.

"Fuck it, Eldred. I went to the address you wrote on that stupid napkin. Three Oh Two One."

"No!" Eldred shouted, and pounded a fist on the console. "Not 'Two One', it's Three Oh *One Two*. You fucked this up, girl. Where did you go to? Who'd you kill?"

Eldred rested a hand on his knife—still sheathed for the moment. A flood of panic swelled in Tedi's throat. No. No. No. Something's wrong. I'm not getting out of this.

"Eldred, wait," she begged. "You must've written the wrong number. Please wait. *Oh!* I've still got the napkin in my purse."

Tedi reached in her purse. The napkin was in there. But so was Digger's pistol. She pulled the trigger. The bullet cut through Eldred's chest side to side and lodged in the hollow space of the truck door.

She tried to shake the ringing from her ears and looked for anyone who might have seen them or heard the shot. Nobody there but ducks, paddling around through a clump of cattails. She took a fat wad of hundreds and twenties from Eldred's front pocket and stuffed the bills in her jeans, afraid the money might fall out the jagged, smoking hole in her purse.

*   *   *

Tedi drove back out Rollins Creek Road for the dog. Couldn't bear the thought of it trapped there—maybe to starve—in that crate. For the second time in two days, she stood over the old woman's body. Who are you? Why has nobody been here? Are you all alone?

"Sorry about all this," she said to the dead woman. "Don't worry about your dog. I'll take good care of her."

She fled south, no destination in mind. Somewhere between Memphis and Little Rock, she pulled off I-40 where two hard-worn women sold barbecue from a rolling pit towed by an old Jeep. She bought two sandwiches and a Dr Pepper and fed one of the sandwiches to the dog, then walked it over to pee in a copse of trees near a broad pasture.

"We need a name for you," she said. The dog looked up from her squat.

"Trixie? Pixie?" Barbecue smoke drifted over them, distracting the dog from Tedi's name search.

"Molly? Holly? Dolly?"

A squirrel chattered and chased one of its tree-mates down a tall hickory. The dog sprinted after them and Tedi marveled at her speed, watched her almost catch one of them near an ancient oak.

"Digger," she said. "Let's call you Digger."

The Jackshit Bastards

WE WERE BASTARDS, my twin sister and I, born in 1964, when there was still such a thing as bastards. Our mother, Vickie Hart, was nine months pregnant and abandoned in Houston. She listed our father on the birth certificates only as "A.S." and refused to speak his name. To her, we were Samuel and Sara Hart.

Our mother used guile and bluff and bare knuckles to keep us alive, the three of us a traveling circus of survival, constantly shifting from one pungent, roach-eaten apartment to another, masters of the perpetual rent-dodge. We skirted the edge of homelessness, but she always managed to pull us back by sharing both shelter and waitress jobs with a series of other chain-smoking, discarded women dragging colicky babies, raging toddlers, and sullen—sometimes dangerous—teenagers in their miserable wake.

By the time we started school, life was a runaway hairball of here-again-gone-again roommates, twenty-four-hour work schedules, go-to-sleep-here-wake-up-there dazes, and bus stop prisoner exchanges.

Gloria will put you to bed. Margie will walk you to the bus. Play quietly so Mommy can sleep. Agnes will be here till three. Wake up honey, I'm going to drop you at Helen's on my way to work. Bella will pick you up after her shift.

Our mother never brought a boyfriend home that I remember, but all the other kids' moms did. They ranged from crew-cut longshoremen to hippie moochers to druggie bikers in and out so quickly, we rarely knew their names. We learned to stay out of their way, or even better, out of their sight. Some of them didn't want grown women. They roamed and hunted among the whirl of kids, the men like feral cats loosed on a clutch of hatchlings.

Sara figured out how to jackshit when the boyfriends showed up, and then she taught it to me. There always seemed to be a toddler around in need of a diaper change, and when Sara first learned this trick the easiest one to catch was a kid named Jackson. How it worked was you corralled Jackson (or whoever) and reached down the back of his diaper and harvested what you could, enough to share, and you smeared it around your neck. A thin smear under the collar all the way around. Unless the men were high or drunk, then you had to lay it on thicker. It didn't always work, of course, but it kept some of them off you.

There was one guy with bad Elvis hair and a shaggy mustache who hung around a lot, smelling like cigarettes and gasoline. Sara and I called him Musty, though not to his face. He had a driller's thick sandpapery hands, and his fingernails and the backs of his hands and forearms seemed permanently stained with burnt motor oil.

Musty was playful with the kids, and we loved it when he played grab monster. He'd get you in a chokehold, tight enough to thrill but not frighten, breathe his acrid breath down your cheek and tickle you crazy, around your nipples or inner thigh, way up high.

For the boys, there was an added feature: the pocketknife. While Musty had you in his grip, he'd take out an oversized Old Timer folding knife from a tattered leather holster on his belt, the handle lined with red-dirt filled cracks. He'd whip the knife between your legs and press upward—the blade closed, but in your kid's mind you could never be sure, that was the kick—and he would say something like, "I'll cut 'em off. You want me to cut 'em off?" He said this as playfully as you can say such a thing. Most of us shrieked with a strange confusion of joy and panic.

The game was best when Musty faked disinterest, sitting on the couch watching TV and waiting for a free meal. We'd run back and forth in front of him, hoping to be chosen. He'd ignore us awhile before snatching a random victim. Then he'd put them in a headlock and rough-nuzzle and grate the back of their neck with mustache and three-day chin stubble. All this before applying the heavy-duty tickles. During one game, he ran his hand down Sara's shorts. After that, she put him on her (jack)shit list and told me to hide with her the next time he came. I should've listened.

He was drunk the night he grabbed me in what I thought was the usual game. Before I sensed something was wrong, he dragged me out the back door of our little shared rental house and into an abandoned, half-collapsed garage, moonlight leaking in through a fractured roof.

Musty sat on a chair and bettered his grip on my neck. I gasped for air. Old Timer came out, open this time, the blade rusty and chipped. He pressed it to my crotch and said, "You pull them britches down, or I'll cut you for real this time." I felt his chest hard against my back as he tightened the stranglehold.

"Don't tell nobody, 'cause I'll cut you and anybody you tell."

I unbuckled my belt slowly, stalling to think, then thrust my neck backwards into his face, smearing jackshit across his lips and nose.

"Fuck!" he shouted, gagging and cussing. He shoved me to the dirt floor, and I shot up and out the door. Sara had smeared it on me a little thicker than usual that night when she heard the distinctive rattle of Musty's truck roll into our driveway.

*   *   *

A few days before we started fourth grade, Mom got us up early and the three of us walked to a Metro bus stop, the morning air as wet and hot as horse breath. We climbed on the bus, our T-shirts sweat-glued to our backs, Mom sitting between us and speaking softly, pointing and commenting about people and cars and billboards along the way. The bus jerked side to side, squeaking as it turned corners deeper and deeper into the Second Ward. When we got off, Mom held our hands and walked us to Casa de Esperanza, a children's home. She sat with us on a bench near the front doors of the Casa and told us she had to go on a trip, and it would be better and safer for us to stay at this place while she was away.

"Don't go inside yet," she said. "I want to wave goodbye from the bus stop."

It took awhile for the bus to come, so Mom did a few practice waves and Sara said, "Stop crying, Sam. You're acting like a titty baby. She's just going to hunt for Daddy. She's going to find A.S."

The Metro came, and she took a window seat facing us and waved the real goodbye wave. Later, the police told the nuns who ran Casa de Esperanza what happened: Mom took the bus a couple of miles to Hidalgo Park and climbed a railroad embankment to the Union Pacific tracks leading downtown. There, she followed the rails a quarter mile to the rusted iron hulk of a swinging railroad bridge, swung open to let ships pass down the black waters of Buffalo Bayou, a hundred feet below. That's where she jumped.

* * *

It's our fiftieth birthday—a zero birthday, a big one. I'm barely out of bed and making coffee when my phone buzzes. I know without looking it's Sara because of our birthday call ritual and sing-along. It's a contest to see who'll call first. She's called me at 12:01 a.m. some years. During her Army years, we couldn't sing on our actual birthday because she couldn't call or be called in the backcountry of Kuwait or Bosnia or South Korea. But we always managed to make up for it, days or weeks later.

Since her return from the Army, we've never been more than an hour's drive apart. I drifted from town to town, from bad job to unemployment check to worse job, but always managed to live close enough to Houston for weekend visits.

I answer my phone, and Sara launches into "Happy Birthday."

"Sara? Is that you? Or is somebody strangling a cat?"

"Oh yeah? Well you're no Michael Bublé."

"Happy damn birthday, Marshal Hart."

After retiring from the Army as an M.P., Sara joined the US Marshals Service and spent the last twelve years tracking down fugitives and body-guarding federal judges.

"Actually," Sara says, "I've given my notice. Margot and I are moving to Brooklyn. Well, Margot's already here. Been up here a couple of weeks now."

"*Here*? Sara, are you in Brooklyn now?"

Dread clamps my gut. I'm losing Sara again. Losing the sane half of me, the half with a candle and a map who knows how to find her way out of a shitstorm. We were inseparable as kids. Never lost touch as adults. Saved each other many times. Now what? Will I be lucky to see her twice a year in hurried visits, after a surprise "hey we're passing through" call? Making do with a tin voice on the phone? Or the cold cardboard of a greeting card staring back at me, the very symbol of *I've got better things to do*?

"Yeah. Up here for a week or so this trip. The full move is next month."

Dammit, Margot. Dragging my sister off to New York. Of all the damn places. Sara and Margot met about two years ago, when Margot interviewed Sara for an *Esquire* piece about female marshals.

"This is the part where you act happy for us," Sara says, shaming me out of silence.

"Wow. I'm just stunned. New York City. Big stuff."

"Netflix bought the film rights to Margot's first novel. They've hired her to do the screenplay. Since the story is set mostly in Brooklyn and Jersey, she wants to be here on the ground—where she grew up—while she's writing."

"Sure. Makes sense," I say, trying to break out of my daze.

Screenplay? Netflix? Margot's doing a movie while I pile up unsold paintings and half-finished sketches around my trailer between bouts of driving a concrete truck part time and cleaning the floors at Home Depot by night. Sara's found what seems like real love (with a much younger woman) and I'm still trawling East Texas honky-tonks and Louisiana casinos, apparently invisible to all women under seventy. Happy birthday to me.

"Sam, fly up this weekend! We need to party. Five-Oh!"

"You know I can't swing that."

"Margot and I are buying."

"I can't let you."

"It's the cost of a plane ticket for heaven's sake. Come on, we've got to do this."

"It feels weird to me, Sara."

"You need to get out of Texas for a while. What's the name of that little backwater mudhole you moved to? White Horse?"

"White Church."

"How do you stay sane?"

"It's not so bad here. We even have internet. It might be powered by a mule on a treadmill, but it still crushes your soul, just like in the big city."

"Wah, wah, wah."

"OK, I'll come to your fancy damn hipster town. On one condition."

"Yeah?"

"I get to meet Jimmy Fallon."

*   *   *

Once a week at La Casa de Esperanza, the potential adopters and fosters would come by and inspect us like appliances on a showroom floor, something they needed to complete their kitchen or laundry room. Sometimes, they moved on to the next store, hoping for better inventory. Maybe something in a different size or color. Some kids got carted off and never came back, but many revolved in and out, a little more damaged by each boomerang cycle.

Sara was always the right size and color. Everyone wanted Sara. Why not? She was whip-smart, calm, and pretty. She was respectful of the nuns (to their faces) and attentive to the browsers, quick to chat them up as they kicked our tires.

Nobody wanted me, though. I was a moody kid who wouldn't make eye contact or talk, and if I did speak, no one could understand my sparse, faint words. I was the boy who wouldn't stop drawing and coloring even when the nuns took away my papers and pencils. When that happened, I kept on drawing in my head.

Of all the bad Esperanza days, the showroom floor days were the worst for me, the days when Sara would be taken. I knew when it was about to happen because Mr. Kirkland the janitor would appear, stinking of piss and Lysol. Kirkland would arrive and shadow me. That was my signal to watch for a nun coming from the girls' hall with Sara's bag. When I saw the bag, I'd sprint to Sara, bawling, and latch both arms and legs around her.

Sara never cried during these separations. She did her little girl motherly best to console me. "Sam, it's OK. Don't worry. Maybe they'll let me call you." These were the words she wanted the nuns to hear. But no one could hear Sara's whispers to me, her lips pressing my ear, "It won't be long. I'll be back. Promise." Sara didn't cry because she had a plan. I cried because I feared each time would be the time her plan didn't work.

Kirkland's job was to help the nuns pry me off my sister, carry me back to my bed in the boys' dorm and block the door. Sister Marina explained it to me one time when Sara left, why I couldn't go with her.

"These things are the result of prayer," she said. "Sara is the answer to that family's prayer."

"I'm not an answer?"

"Sure you are. You're just the answer to a prayer no one has prayed."

Then she gave me my drawing stuff back.

Sara brought herself back to me every time. Some families taking her were good and some were bad, but even the bad ones were a vacation for her if they had the pleasures not allowed at Esperanza, like television or junk food. Or schools without nuns. Sara played along with each new family for a week or so, then she would monkey-wrench something. Scissor the curtains. Key a car. Steal money. Boomerang: we're back together.

One of the last families to take Sara on a trial run were the wealthy Teasdales, from Austin. She was gone too long and I panicked. The plan clearly wasn't working. I spent every minute the nuns would allow watching out a window overlooking the front driveway to Esperanza, hoping to see my sister step out of a Mercedes or Cadillac and rejoin me in Nunland. All that month, no Sara.

Her stunts to get kicked back to Esperanza weren't working, Sara explained later, because the Teasdales were too damn nice. They were gentle and kind to Sara, and very generous. They lived in what Sara described as a mansion next to a big park, with its own duck lake and tennis court. Deer grazed in front of the house every morning. She had her own bedroom, and also a connecting room—almost as large as the bedroom—for toys. A room *only* for toys!

When Sara decided it was time to come back to me, she went to the greenhouse with a pair of scissors and clear-cut an entire pallet of rare orchids Mrs. Teasdale had spent years cross-pollinating. The woman cried over her lost treasures, but hugged Sara. "It's OK, honey. You didn't know how important they were. Let me explain it to you."

A few days later, during a backyard pool party, Sara sneaked into the house and pulled the drainplugs on a giant aquarium in the study. The fancy carpet was soaked with stinking water by the time Mr. Teasdale found the mess, his exotic fish scattered and gasping. Sara walked in and handed him the plugs. He never raised his voice or hit her, just told her to never touch the aquarium again without permission, then sent her to time-out in her bedroom and toy annex. At that point, Sara said, she thought she might be stuck there.

But Sara was the grandmaster of Plan B. One morning before school, she took a razor blade from the crafts room and sliced an "S" into her inner forearm. She let it get good and bloody before going down to join the family for breakfast. That move backfired, because instead of a return trip to Esperanza, she landed in the office of the best child shrink in Austin.

Sara's therapy didn't last long. Soon after the "S" on her arm, she took a pushpin from the kitchen bulletin board and cut a "T" into the belly of Tylee McCallum, the toddler from next door. The Teasdales drove her back to Esperanza the following afternoon.

The nuns figured Sara out after a while. One kindly nun, Sister Isabel, took pity and tried but failed to push us as a "package deal" to several couples, hoping to defuse Sara's return-to-sender ploys. It never worked. No one wants a racehorse, even a prize one, if it has to drag a mule around the track. Besides, Sara's bait-and-switch reputation caught up with her, especially as she got older, so there were fewer and fewer takers anyway.

We had an unspoken pact: better to live a crummy life together than for only one of us to escape. This pact doomed us to Esperanza. And doomed Sara to dragging a mule.

*   *   *

One predawn morning, shortly after turning fifteen, I went out a window on the second floor of the boys' dorm with some survival items in a book bag and fire-poled down a drainpipe to spongy wet grass. Sara waited for me at the bus stop across the street, the last place we'd seen our mother. From there, we left Esperanza behind, running to—well, we didn't know where—all we knew was we were doing it together.

Shoplifting kept us fed. Abandoned buildings and empty houses sheltered us, as long as we kept moving. We learned how to cheat at street games of dice and cards without getting stabbed. We met a junkie called Birdie who was always good for twenty bucks or so, especially when she had the shakes and couldn't focus. When Birdie was like that, she couldn't catch Sara switching the dice when it was time to pluck her. Being twitchy and loopy made Birdie insanely hopeful, rolling the bones over and over. Never winning but always hoping.

Birdie was friends with Cal, a middle-aged ex-con who ran the biggest chop shop operation in Houston. At first, Cal came across more like a country preacher than a violent criminal. But as you got to know him, his soft voice and constant smile did little to hide the thug within. And he always stared at Sara. I hated the way he watched her, the way a lion watches a zebra.

Cal didn't do dice, which was great because nobody would survive cheating him. We were too smart to try. But we weren't smart enough to say no when Cal recruited us to steal cars. He taught us the skills and paid fifty bucks for "choppers" (the ones they dismantled for parts) and anywhere from a hundred to two fifty for "shippers," depending on value. Shippers were high-end cars worth more whole than in pieces, so Cal's team reprocessed them with new VIN numbers and fake papers and rolled them onto ships bound for Mexico or South America.

It was easy money for a couple of rogue teenagers. We could snag two or three cars a night, which got us away from sleeping in condemned houses and into an apartment (with Cal's help as our "dad" signing a fake name to the lease).

And the risk was low because back then nobody had a telephone in their pocket. If a guy comes out of a strip club after midnight and his hot Trans Am is gone, he's got to go back inside the club or find a pay phone somewhere. By then, Sara and I would have his car parked in a warehouse behind another warehouse somewhere in the boonies of the Houston ship channel.

* * *

I'm late landing at LaGuardia, so instead of meeting Sara and Margot at their apartment in Brooklyn, I take a cab to the restaurant for our birthday dinner. It's a French bistro called Savourer. This has to be Margot's doing; Sara would've gone Thai or Mexican. The place is small and casual (thank God) but classy, and located near the Theater District, wedged between a pharmacy and a coffee house, and directly across the street from a bookstore.

The bookstore occupies all four floors of a black brick building, with large bay windows framing the entrance at street level. I'm here at dusk. Soft golden light pools out the bay windows into the street. A rusty sign—shaped like a sperm whale—hangs across the entrance between the windows: *Ishmael's Books & More*.

I spot Sara and Margot at a sidewalk table. Sara waves.

"Sam! Over here."

"Sorry about the plane," I say as we hug.

"No worries," Margot says, and offers a hug. I don't like to hug Margot because she's gorgeous, and when she touches me a jolt shoots through my bones, and I have to suppress the impulse to picture her naked. We pantomime a hug, barely glancing shoulders.

"How are you, Tex?" Margot asks.

"Oh, I'm fine. *Jersey Girl*." Margot grins and softly punches me in the chest, and we laugh as a petite server with pigtails approaches. Her name tag reads "Zena."

"Merlot, sir?" Zena asks, hovering the bottle over my glass.

"Sure." I take a sip and glance across the street toward Ishmael's. A taxi stops curbside, and a woman with two young children get out and skitter under the whale and into the store. Then another taxi—this time three kids and a nanny pop out.

Zena sets the wine bottle down and refills Margot's ice water.

"Whoa," I say. "Margot. No red? Don't you usually have a glass or three?"

"Early meeting tomorrow. Gotta be sharp."

"Movie stuff?" I ask.

"First round of script notes from the producers. I'm scared as hell."

After dinner, over birthday cake delivered tableside by a guy on a Vespa (thank you, Margot), Sara reaches into a bag beside her chair and hands me a shallow box, gift wrapped in random comic book pages.

"Happy birthday!"

"No," I say. "You know we don't do this. We swore a blood oath."

"I know, I know." Sara says, letting a little too much East Texas accent leak in, her letter "I" coming out "Ah." The two of us are on the outer edge of buzzed. One more red will likely push us over.

I tear through pages of Batman, Wonder Woman, and Spiderman until I'm down to a bare manuscript box. Sara chuckles and does a little Merlot sway. Margot holds Sara's hand and nuzzles her cheek, and they giggle like first graders in devious anticipation. I half expect a frog to jump out.

I open the box, and I'm stunned because it holds the only ember of true joy from our time at Casa de Esperanza. It's one of a short series of comic books Sara and I made together. Sara wrote the stories, and I did the drawings. We made only four or five issues because it was too hard hiding them from the nuns.

"Issue #3," I whisper through a fog of wine and the shock of being sucked back in time. I lift this treasure gently from the box. Sara's done it up right: It's in a clear envelope like they use for rare, valuable comics. I tilt it into the streetlight for a better look with one hand, and wipe tears with the other.

"Ass-Man #3," Sara says. We named our protagonist Ass-Man. He started out as A.S.-Man, after the mystery father initials on our birth certificates. But we were kids, so naturally we went vulgar and A.S.-Man turned into Ass-Man. I drew his head as a pair of bulbous butt cheeks with big googly eyes, and a little round pink mouth. Right in the middle. He had the required tight-fitting suit and a cape emblazoned with "A.S." He even had a catchphrase when he launched into flight: *Ass-Man Forever!*

"Where on earth, Sara? Where . . . ?"

"I stored a footlocker at Fort Hood before my first deployment. When I came back a year later, it had been shipped off as unclaimed property to a warehouse God knows where."

"We got a letter from the DOD about a month ago," Margot says. "Somebody decided the old lockers belonged to dead soldiers. So, they traced the names to return belongings to the families."

"And abracadabra," I say. "Ass-Man returns to us. Best birthday ever!" I look around for Zena, to order champagne I can't afford.

"Actually—it's not over," Sara says before I can locate Zena.

"Not by a long shot," Margot chimes in, and shifts back in her chair. Zena emerges from inside Savourer, and Margot signals for the check. A limo arrives at Ishmael's, ferrying two couples and another gaggle of kids. Other parents with children are pouring in on foot—from deep inside the Theater District proper, from back toward Times Square.

Sara stands and bobbles before stepping around to my side of the little table and crouches next to me. She cradles my arm in her hands and presses her face into my shoulder for a second.

"A.S. is here. Ass-Man is here," Sara says.

Her words stupefy me. Have we hit our Merlot limit, because I'm thinking Sara must be drunk? *What the hell is she talking about?* I turn to Margot for a clue, squinting at her in confusion, but she pretends to check her phone, avoiding me.

"What do you mean, Ass-Man is here?" I say, giving a confused, nervous half laugh. "From our comic book?"

It has to be a prank. I scan up and down the sidewalk and over my shoulder. Have they hired some caped costume guy to show up and sing "Happy Birthday"? But Sara's never done a prank, and her face is as straight and serious as a gravestone.

"Our father. *A.S.* from the birth certificates. He's *there.*" Sara points at Ishmael's. I'm shocked to see tears creeping down her cheeks. I haven't seen Sara cry since our earliest days at Esperanza.

"Sara, you're not making any sense," I say. "What? Who? I don't understand what's happening . . ." I fumble with my words like a dimwit.

"I found our father," Sara says, wiping her face.

It's a sucker-punch, numbing me for a minute, so much blood surging into my head I can barely hear the outside world. It's hard to say what hurts most: hearing our sorry father is still alive or being duped by Sara.

"Why the holy *fuck* would you do that?" I don't wear anger for Sara well. It feels like a borrowed funeral suit, something sad and ugly and ill-fitting.

"That's what US Marshals do. We find people."

"She worked hard tracking him down. For months," Margot says.

"He works there?" I spit the words, jabbing a finger toward Ishmael's.

"He's doing a reading there tonight," Margot says.

"A *reading*? What the hell?" I say.

"Your father . . ." Margot begins.

"No! *Not* our father!" I shout at Margot.

"He—the man over there who's about to read his new book—he's Jules Louvette," Margot barks back. Like I'm supposed to know who that is.

Louvette, Louvette. That name is somehow familiar. Then I flash on it. Of course. The kids. Why so many kids are streaming into Ishmael's.

"You mean the guy who writes all the children's books? And the TV specials? *Ralph the Reindeer* every year at Christmas?" I'm incredulous.

"And *Betsy the Bat* at Halloween," Margot says.

"*Betsy the* fucking *Bat* guy is our father? Lord God."

"Those specials have been running over twenty years now," Margot says. "He's the narrator. And executive producer. Top ten in ratings every year." These facts seem to delight Margot. I glare at her, my face pinched and hands raised in disgust that she knows so much about this jerk.

"What?" Margot says, wagging her phone at me. "Google."

"His real name is Alvin Scraggs," Sara says. "He's seventy-five. Born and raised in Kilgore, Texas. After he abandoned Mom in sixty-four, he ended up in Europe. Changed his name to Jules Louvette."

"Well, you have to admit, Alvin Scraggs is not the most artsy name," Margot says.

"I know what's going on here now," I say, stabbing my steak knife through the cardboard box holding leftover cake. "We're sitting on a sidewalk in hell. All this time, I thought we were doing a little birthday, but no, we are actually sitting in fucking hell. There's really no other explanation."

"I know it doesn't make sense to you, but I want us to see him," Sara says, red-eyed, her makeup ruined. She rakes through her purse for tissues.

"Sam," Margot whisper-shouts at me. Then she lips the word "please," cuts her eyes at Sara and jerks her chin toward Ishmael's.

"No goddamn way," I say, struggling to keep my voice down and my words slow and measured. I'm furious at how Sara and Margot have played me. They knew I'd never come to New York if they had been honest about their plans. I bolt from my chair, the metal legs sparking across the concrete before it crashes over backwards, almost hitting a hipster and his date as they pass by. He shouts *asshole* at me, so I give the chair a defiant kick in his direction as I stalk into Savourer, looking for the bar.

By the time Sara finds me sulled up in the bar, I've downed one bourbon, with another coming.

"That was a shitty trick," I say to Sara, trying not to look at her as she sidles in. The overly muscled bartender delivers my second bourbon and Sara orders an IPA.

"I thought it might help us," Sara says. "Help put a lot of crap behind us. You know. Face the dragon. Put that final nail in the coffin of our childhood."

"I left all my wooden stakes and silver bullets at home."

Sara leans around to look me in the eye, so close I can smell her perfume mixed with garlic from the snails she and Margot shared. I stare straight ahead, but she takes my face in both hands, her hands as cold as the granite bar top, and she gently turns my head until we're eye to eye. Just the way she did when we were kids, and I was lost and overwhelmed and needed retrieving.

"I've got a badge and a Glock in my purse," she whispers mischievously, grinning. "I don't need no stinking silver bullets. I got hollow points."

The tears come to me now, goddamn it. I shake and slump and Sara steps off her stool and wraps me in a bear hug. The bartender swings by and discreetly slips a short stack of bar napkins in front of us. I take one and wipe snot, then clench my jaw and try as hard as I can to stop crying in public.

"Margot's pregnant," Sara says.

"I knew it!" I say. The tears ebb, and I feel the first flush of forgiveness for Sara's sneaky trap.

"She skipped wine!" I shout. Sara nods and laughs.

"Margot never skips wine, come on!" I say. "And she ate at least five thousand calories tonight. Oink." Sara pounds the bar and guzzles her beer.

"It's great news, Sara. A real family!" I hug her neck.

"A real family," she says. We click glasses, the last thirty-six hours making a little more sense now.

"Is this why you tracked down Ass-Man? Some newfound maternal drive to dig up roots? Connect with ol' Grandpappy? I doubt any good will come from it, Sis."

"Good or bad doesn't really matter," Sara says. "My life has been police and military. My sworn enemies are loose ends and missing puzzle pieces. I can't walk away tonight knowing he's just across that little, narrow street.

This close." She holds her thumb and forefinger a fraction apart in front of my nose. "We've got to see what's there. Otherwise, I'll never sleep again."

I fear Sara's looking for a speck of connection or acknowledgment where none exists. It's probably a bad idea, but we've survived bad ideas before. As a team. I can't let her do this alone. I owe her too much.

"All I know is cops need backup. So, I'll let you drag me over there. But not because I give two shits about this guy. I'm doing it for you. Only for you."

*   *   *

The last night I worked for Cal, I went out alone because Sara was sick in bed. One of Cal's guys dropped me in a suburban neighborhood where I jacked an F-150 Ford pickup parked in front of a nice home. F-150s were always in high demand for their parts. But this one had a bad taillight. I was within ten minutes of the drop location when a highway patrol car eased up behind me on I-610 and flipped on its lights.

If Sara had been with me, she would have told me to pull over because she was cool under pressure, curvy and smiley, a real snake charmer. She would have spun some BS story about joyriding. They might have detained us for a while, but no real harm done.

But when I saw the cop's lights, I gunned the F-150. Got up to almost a hundred and zigged around an eighteen-wheeler. Then tried to zag around another one, lost control and hit a car on the shoulder where two men were changing a tire. Killed one of them.

I was an adult for criminal purposes in Texas, and was convicted of several crimes, but the worst was manslaughter in the commission of a felony. That got me seven years at the Hornby Unit of the Texas prison system.

My conviction crushed Sara. She came to Hornby on the first visitor's day after I arrived. She forced a smile through the scarred plexiglass, but only her sadness and fear reached me. I was in no shape to lift her mood. I was terrified.

"I'm so sorry," I said. I'd fucked us up and the shame overwhelmed me. I couldn't look her in the face without tears, and the animals at Hornby had already marked me as a weak bunny. Crying would make it worse.

"I'm talking to Cal," Sara said. "Trying to pull enough money together for a real lawyer. Maybe get a reduced sentence." She was pale and drained, in need of a month's sleep.

"No. Forget Cal," I pleaded. "For lawyer money, you'll have to do a lot worse than jacking cars."

"I can do that," she said.

I shook my head, looking away. Sara was pretending, for my sake, that she didn't know the full truth about Cal. He was into a lot more than paying teens to steal cars. Birdie told us things. He had cartel connections and was trafficking girls.

"Listen to me carefully," Sara said, tapping the glass. "I'll do *whatever* it takes to get you out." Her hard, resigned look scared me cold, like she was ready to nut-kick the devil.

"No. Fuck no," I said. This was Cal's opening to swoop in, banking on her being panicked and worried about me. He'd be full of ideas for her to raise cash.

"Don't make me say it," I said.

"Say what?"

"Cal wants to fuck you, that's what. Then probably pass you around to his partners." The thought of it roiled my guts, like shards of glass boring their way out.

"You don't think I know that? I can use that," Sara said, poker-faced.

"God no, Sara! You want to help me? Then I'm begging you. Get away from him."

She stared into her lap, hair falling over her face. Silent.

"I'm begging because I'll die in here unless my head's right. And I can't get it right if I spend every day worrying about you tangled up in Cal's shit. Promise me, Sara."

"And go where? Do what?"

I didn't have an answer. But her getting away from Cal seemed like the only way to save us both.

"You'll think of something. You always do."

A guard told us to wrap it up. Sara mouthed "I love you" and hung up the handset. I wasn't sure I'd convinced her. I was never entirely sure with Sara. As she walked out the door, I wanted to run and cinch my arms and legs around her like all those times at Esperanza. I wanted to hear her secret whisper: *It won't be long. I'll be back. Promise.*

Three days later, on our eighteenth birthday, she joined the Army. Two years after that, she was guarding captured Cuban soldiers in Grenada, and I was recovering in the prison hospital with a splintered leg (twelve pins) and a shattered skull (metal plate) after a skinhead named Lonnie Lee Wray piledrove me into a concrete pillar. I owed him a juice.

* * *

We enter Ishmael's and follow the chatter to the reading room at the back of the first floor. We've missed the reading, but not the book signing, and take our place at the end of the line.

Margot is the first to get a good look at him.

"Dear God," she says. "He looks just like that beer guy."

"Beer guy?" I ask.

"You know, *'The most interesting man in the world.'* The original guy in those Dos Equis commercials? Very, very handsome. Too bad they dumped him for that younger, douchey guy."

She's right, dammit. He could be the beer guy's better-looking brother. Thick pewter hair, swept straight back. Trim, Van Dyke beard and precision-cut suit. *I don't always abandon my family, but when I do, I become a fucking multimillionaire.*

The wait is long, but we're on a mission and finally make it to the table where Ass-Man is signing books with an assistant by his side. Ishmael's has strung a fifty-foot banner behind him: *Jules Louvette: The Voice America Grows Up With* (*Time Magazine*).

I want to puke. Where was he, I wonder, when Sara nearly died of a sniper wound in a dirty, fucking Army tent in Kuwait? Maybe sipping a Kir Royale somewhere near the Louvre? And then, when Lonnie Lee Wray was slapping his fat cock across my face at the Hornby Unit? Maybe lunching with a fellow *artiste* on roasted squab or some such shit?

Sara and I step up to the table.

His assistant readies a copy of his newest picture book and asks, "How would you like it inscribed?"

I've been running the words through my head during the long wait in line.

"Make it out *'To my little bastards,'*" I say. "And have him sign it *'Alvin Scraggs.'*"

Ass-Man winces and slides his reading glasses to the tip of his nose. Walls his eyes up at us.

"*What* did you say?" he asks.

"Vicki Hart. Houston. Nineteen sixty-four," Sara says.

"Ring any bells?" I ask.

"Do I know you?"

"We're relatives," Sara says. "From Texas. Can we talk a few minutes?"

Ass-Man stares at us a long moment, then tells his assistant to give us some privacy. Margot follows the assistant to the front of the store and feigns browsing. Without asking, I drag two folding chairs over, and Sara and I sit across from him at the signing table.

"You know Vicki Hart?" he asks. It's obvious we got his attention with our name-dropping.

"Our mother," Sara says.

"Vicki, my God. So long ago. How *is* she?" he asks.

"Not so good," I say.

"Dead," Sara says. "Four decades now."

"Oh. I had no idea." His face drops a shade of tan.

"Is your father alive?" he asks Sara.

"We believe so," Sara says. "We believe we're looking at him."

"*We?*" he says, leaning back in his chair.

"We're twins," I say.

"Hmm," Ass-Man says, fingering his fancy signing pen and thinking.

"*Money!*" he says at last, dropping the pen and bringing his hands together in a silent clap. "That must be it—you're looking for money. How many people have claimed to be my children over the years? A common scam with men like me."

"No money," I say.

Ignoring me, he begins gathering his things to leave. He thinks he can swat us away. He's wrong. Sara scoots her chair forward and leans on the table.

"You lived in Houston in the early sixties," Sara says. "You were an art student three blocks down from the bar where our mother worked as a waitress. You and Mom dated in sixty-three and four. The owner of the bar remembers you and Mom together and her getting pregnant. Our birth certificates record the father as A.S. Your real name is Alvin Scraggs."

His eyes fix first on me, then on Sara, examining our faces.

"Look, I'm not going to acknowledge anything here," he says and tugs on his little beard. "Maybe Vicki was pregnant from our relationship. Or maybe not."

Sara squints at him and cocks her head.

"And maybe you two are just a couple of redneck grifters," he says with a brief smirk.

Sara shakes her head no, but I explode.

"You're the only phony here, pretty boy!" I shout. "I bet if I jerk that eight-thousand-dollar suit off your ass and shake you real good, we'll see some East Texas red dirt come falling out your butt crack."

I'm standing over him, but I don't remember standing, and my voice seems to be coming from somewhere outside myself, like I'm hearing some unseen stranger losing his shit around the corner.

"She's a hero," I say, lowering my voice a notch but still too loud, pointing at Sara. "She's going to be a mother soon, and her kid is going to look at her and see a goddamn hero. No one is ever going to look at you or me and see that."

Shaking, I sit. Elbows on my knees, head in hands. *Please God no one call the police.* Sara reaches over and gently strokes the back of my neck.

Ass-Man raises a single finger above the tabletop. "A one-time payment with no admission of anything by me," he says. "For you to go away. You'll have to sign a non-disclosure. Absolutely no press."

Sara bows her head and briefly closes her eyes. Her quiet tears cut into me.

"We really didn't come for money," she says, her voice cracking.

"No? What then?" He raises his voice, pushing us, looking to end this bad evening. The three of us sit in a long, boiling silence.

Sara needs something to come from this. There's a showy display of Louvette merchandise nearby: T-shirts, coffee mugs, ball caps and over-priced trinkets of all kinds. And books, shelves and shelves of Louvette picture books. I walk to the shelves and run my finger down a long row of narrow spines, picking one at random: *Pixie the Pig*.

I hand it to him.

"Here."

"What?"

"Read us this."

"You're kidding."

"Just read the damn book. Then we'll go."

"Really? You'll go?"

"Forever," I say. "Can't wait."

He pauses and fans the book's pages, his face a mix of surprise and bemusement as he mulls my offer.

"Deal," he says finally, and lifts a palm in agreement and relief.

He admires the book's cover a moment and begrudgingly holds it up for us to see. I want to hate it more than I want to breathe, but his art is magnificent. Two human-like pigs, an adult wearing a church-lady hat holding hands with a juvenile, walk along a winding path cutting through dark undergrowth. The forest is intricate and Paleozoic, a riot of fronds, limbs, branches and leaves, rendered in emerald, olive, turquoise and teal and other shades of green I've never seen, accented with silvers and grays and blacks. The pigs are plump and curvy, Rubenesque. And so shockingly pink, Pepto pink, they blur off the page.

Ass-Man clears his throat and sips some tea and wraps his honeyed TV voice—*The Voice America Grows Up With*—around the story. Sara leans in, but not me. I drift away. Drift into the never-was. Where Alvin never left and Mom never went to that bridge. A place with bedtime stories. A place without jackshit.

An Arm and a Prayer

IT WAS A HINDU, not a Christian, who gave me a new arm. This happened despite the best efforts of my aunt, Sunshine Bastrop. I called her Sunny. She fought hard for my new arm to be a miracle from Jesus. If I had been lame or blind, or even comatose, her efforts might have worked. At least according to the Sunday morning TV preachers she sent money, money we couldn't spare. But a new arm? Their weepy donation-driven miracles couldn't conjure that level of magic.

I was in third grade when she invited Brother Howard Granger for a visit. No, he wasn't a TV preacher. I doubt he even owned a television.

I knew something was up when Sunny opened the door when he knocked. Our usual reaction to people at the door was to hide in her bedroom closet and attempt to pray the intruders away, usually Jehovah's Witnesses or smarmy life insurance salesmen.

"I'm here to help you pray for the boy," he said, a dusty black Stetson in hand, loose turkey skin jangling around his Adam's apple.

He was thin and stern-faced with salt-and-pepper hair cut unevenly, like he'd run out of money halfway through. He said he was starting a new church in Conifer, the little East Texas town ten miles from where we lived on a lonely stretch of US Hwy 271, our only neighbors being scattered stands of loblolly pines and forlorn cattle.

The preacher and I sat alone in our tiny living room while Sunny got Cokes. He didn't speak while she was in the kitchen, but focused intently on the empty right sleeve of my sweatshirt, where Sunny had folded it over and pinned it. It was typical for people to look for a few seconds, then avert their eyes. Brother Granger's eyes lingered on my emptiness. A long, hard, hungry stare.

"Jesus Christ can give the boy his arm back," he said, and slurped the Coke. Sunny sat on the opposite end of the couch from him, her heft pressing a mournful croak from the springs and frame. Had the couch been a seesaw, she would have popped Granger into the air. She lit a Camel and studied the man.

"If you truly believe, anything is possible," he said. "Have you accepted Christ, Mizz Bastrop?" He fixed his small, dark eyes on her, unblinking and merciless. A challenge.

"You think Ah'm a goddamn atheist? Shiiiiiit," she said, twisting her head sideways, blowing smoke. "Nobody loves the Good Lord more than Ah do. You can bet your lily-white ass on that."

"Praise be, Mizz Bastrop. Praise be." He trained his snakish eyes on me.

"Boy, take that shirt off. Let's see what the Devil's done."

I turned to Sunny, and she nodded. She grabbed my left sleeve and pulled the shirt off. Granger reached for my scars, but I twisted away impulsively, violently, as if escaping a scorpion or big hairy spider.

"Don't you believe, boy? Or not?" His words boomed at me.

"Yes. No. What?" I said, wanting desperately to run out the door and down the highway. "Billy Wayne Bastrop!" Sunny shouted and stubbed out her Camel. She glared at me.

I was embarrassing her in front of the holy man.

I couldn't help it. I felt completely naked in front of the rough, grizzled stranger. No one other than Sunny had seen the truth of me. The scars at the top of my right shoulder, the scars that marked where my arm departed this world, were the most intimate, shameful, and sacred part of me. Much more so than my genitals. I sobbed and sank to the floor.

"Shit fire, Billy," Sunny said. "Git your ass up off the rug and let this man help you. Let the power and love of Jesus come into you." There was no stopping it. The two of them were a team now.

"Let me lay the healing hands on you, Billy." This time his voice was as inviting as he could make it, but still held a whiff of menace—scary-sweet—like syrup flowing across shards of glass.

He put both hands around the top of my right arm socket. The coldness of his hands cut through my body, the chill shooting down my spine and into my toes. And as he prayed to Jesus to grow me another arm, his acrid breath wormed down my throat.

He laid on the hands a few moments at a time, almost knocking me to the floor, then broke away and mumbled to himself and slouched as if exhausted, then laid the hands on again. He did this three times, led us in a long, rambling prayer, then announced he had to go, to prepare a sermon.

"Bring the boy to services Sunday," he said to Sunny as they stood on the porch.

"Y'all handle?" she asked.

Granger brightened and cockeyed her, gave a brief, faint smile and said, "Oh my yes, Mizz Bastrop. Just like the Good Book says, Mark 16: *'they will pick up serpents with their hands.'*" Sunny almost beamed, a rare and curious expression for her.

"Are you *that* strong of faith, ma'am? Do you handle?"

"Ain't done it in forever. But Ah can take it back up. If you think it'll help the boy."

Granger clasped his hands and did a victorious pump. "It always helps to be of strong faith, Mizz Bastrop. Always."

As he left, she gave him fifty dollars for his ministry, which meant nothing but beans and corn bread for us that week. And never mind ice cream. Thankfully, we didn't go to his Sunday services because Sunny said she couldn't stand to be around a bunch of holy rollers for two hours. Besides, she said, the assholes don't allow smoking.

For the next couple of months, the preacher stopped by on random afternoons. During these visits, he admonished her for not coming to his new church, The Church of All Truth. Then he repeated the laying-on-of-hands ceremony to grow me a new arm.

When it was apparent nothing much was happening, Sunny got tighter with the money until one day Brother Granger pointed at some scar tissue and convinced her the smooth, shiny bumps of skin were the beginnings of new fingers protruding from the top of my shoulder. He scored a healthy donation that day but still eventually stopped coming, either disgusted by my lack of faith, or maybe just knew when to drop a scam that had run its course. I knew the man liked snakes. I think they were his kin.

*   *   *

It must have been tiresome for Sunny—a never-married, childless, fiftyish woman—thrust into reluctant motherhood. In those first couple of years—she took me in when I was four—I pestered her constantly about my missing family. It wasn't that I enjoyed hearing about my family's ruin, like a kid transfixed by the umpteenth reading of *Green Eggs and Ham*; I just kept hoping the story of Billy and his lost family, in at least one of the recitations, would have a different end.

But the story never changed: car wreck, sister Lucy dead, arm gone. A family blinked away by fate on a blacktop road. My mother Julia poured her blood down a rusty bathtub drain, unable to cope with Lucy's death and my mutilation. My father Cecil—Sunshine's brother—apparently less courageous than my mother, loaded a pickup with the tools of his mechanic's trade and vanished into distant memory, erasing me from his life.

I thought of them constantly, my missing pieces. Drew a hundred crayon pictures, Sunny sitting on the floor with me at the coffee table—a daring feat given her size—holding the paper because I couldn't steady the paper *and* color with only one hand. She'd bring in Fritos and queso and giant slices of pecan pie and watch me color away at Mama's dress, Lucy's long hair, Daddy waving from his truck.

"They're not gone forever," Sunny kept telling me, taping my best work to the fridge. "You'll see them when you get to heaven."

"My arm too?"

She groaned, pondering the question.

"Ah don't know why not. The Lord probably ain't got nothing against your arm."

If prayer couldn't give me my arm back, I reasoned, there was certainly no retrieving the dead. But my father Cecil was another matter. He was alive somewhere, as far as we knew, but never any cards or letters. Or phone calls.

I decided he wanted to come back but couldn't, because he was being held in an enemy prison, captured as a spy. Or hit his head and had amnesia and was stranded on a South Pacific island. I imagined him as a covert astronaut on his way to Jupiter, part of a top-secret U.N. mission to save the world. Could it be he was a time traveler? Chained in the dungeon of a medieval castle?

I built an ever-growing wall of movie-trope explanations around my heart to block out the darker, more venomous possibilities:

He didn't want me.

He never wanted me.

He especially didn't want the one-armed me.

* * *

The Hindu I spoke of was Dr. Vijay Mallick, a pediatric prosthetics specialist in Dallas. Sunny and I left for our appointment with him shortly after sunrise on an overcast day in late November, three days before my ninth birthday. It was a long drive. About two packs of Camels long.

Sunny was against it. Mrs. Finch, my school nurse, after much cursing (Sunny), name calling (again, Sunny), and tears (me and Mrs. Finch), convinced Sunny to take me to Dr. Mallick. Finch called to make the appointment so Sunny could be spared talking to anyone, and drew us a map with the doctor's name, address, and phone number written across the top. The nurse also made a brilliant but risky move: She listed the doctor's name only as V. J. (not Vijay) Mallick, and made no mention to Sunny of the fact he was Indian. I had my fingers crossed the whole way hoping Sunny would make no associations with the name "Mallick."

We had no problem finding Dallas, since we just pointed Sunny's glowing red traveling lips west on I-30, listening to the radio reception getting better and better as we got closer to the city, the country songs clearer, reports of the president's planned visit that day cutting in from time to time.

Once in the city, however, we got lost three times before locating Dr. Mallick's office two blocks north of downtown, between Big D Used Cars and Lester's Mustang Lounge. Mallick's office was in what appeared to be a former gas station, or possibly a muffler shop, with the reception area located in the cash-register part of the building, and the examining rooms, X-ray equipment, and prosthesis display rooms in what used to be the garage bays.

There was no one in the waiting room. No patients, no receptionist behind the small battleship-gray metal desk. Sunny forced her ample butt into a green vinyl chair and poked another Camel into her still-slippery, but now fading scarlet lips. I sat beside her, thrilled by a stack of *National Geographics* a foot high on the side table.

Sunny had the room well smoked when a perfectly proportioned, obsidian-haired, caramel-skinned woman swept into the reception area. Her gorgeous hair was long, and twirled and folded up on the back of her head, every strand precisely placed. She wore an ankle-length dress of shiny burnt-orange cloth, expertly wrapped, showing her figure to be Greek-statue classic: delicate shoulders, moderate bust, narrow waist, graceful hips, long slim legs. A red dot rested between her black eyebrows. You always remember a moment like this: the exact moment you fall in love for the first time.

The woman floated over to her ugly metal desk, an incredibly unfitting place for her to be, like a swan assigned to a rusted washtub.

"Be-lee Bahs-troop," she said melodically, addressing me and smiling. Drilling deeper into my heart.

"Yes, ma'am," I responded. Should I call her ma'am? That didn't seem quite adequate.

"The name's Bastrop, not Bahs-troop." Sunny's stone-tongue drawl came through a haze of smoke and startled me. For a minute, I'd forgotten I was with her walrus-ness.

"Quite sorry," the Indian lady said to Sunny. "I must tell Dr. Mallick you are here." She vanished in a swish of cloth and a hint of spice. I liked it here. I liked it here a lot.

"Now wouldn't that frost your balls!" Sunny folded both meaty arms across the barrels of her breasts, loose flesh hanging from her armpits almost to her elbows. She leaned her head back and exhaled enough smoke to finish filling the room with a stinking cloud.

"GD foreigners! And that stupid shit-for-brains, stupid-ass school nurse. Why didn't she tell us?" Tears welled in Sunny's eyes. She gave me a pity-ing look, a look asking me to forgive her for leading us into some kind of trap. With authentic fear, she leaned over to me and whisper-shouted, "They're spies, you know they're spies!"

"Be-lee! Be-lee!" Dr. Vijay Mallick burst into the room, followed by the graceful receptionist—so easy in her movements, effortlessly matching the doctor's rapid pace. The doctor was small and lithe, no taller than Sunny. He moved everywhere in a hurry and talked faster than anyone I had ever met, always using more words than necessary to make his point.

"Please now Be-lee, please now, you and your mother come back to room number three. Yes, room number three it shall be." He waved his hands, as if he could create an air current strong enough to sweep us into the correct room.

"Ah'm not his mama. Ah'm his aint." Sunny announced as we entered the exam room. She was almost shouting—which amped up her drawl— as if Dr. Mallick was deaf and mentally challenged.

"I am so sorry, Mrs. Bash-trap, but please forgive me for not maybe understanding you, but . . ." his eyes shot back and forth at Sunny and me, clearly embarrassed, "but you are saying you are *a saint*?"

He squinted, his smile forced and nervous. Sunny sneered and moved back two steps, curling her upper fluorescent lip. She raised her voice even more.

"Holy hell! Shit no, Ah'm no goddamn Catholic. Ah'm the boy's aint, Ah'm telling you. Billy's my *nephew*. NAY-FEW."

With this, Sunny skulked to the window, exhaling smoke at shafts of sunlight that briefly crossed her broad face. She muttered something unintelligible—but you can bet hot and nasty—toward the glass.

"Yes, yes, of course. I see now. Be-lee, this is your aunt. You are the *nephew*. Very good."

"Yessir." I was terrified Sunny would gather me up and bolt from Mallick's office in a snit. If I was lucky, maybe he would send Sunny back to the front, to keep the pretty woman company. I couldn't leave Dallas without an arm. I was desperate for it, to take a first step toward normalcy.

To move away from the other-ness I felt everywhere and every day. But most importantly, I needed it to get my daddy back.

"Be-lee, please take off your blouse. I will return soon. Blouse and under garment off, OK?" He darted out like a cat. Sunny dropped her gaze-out-the-window ruse and shut the door behind him.

"Dr. Whatzit there must think you're a girl. *Take off your blouse, Billy,*" she mocked him, but didn't attempt the accent.

"Some people call shirts blouses, Sunny. He didn't mean anything by it. I read that in my geography book." I unbuttoned my shirt as I spoke, and as I reached the last button, Sunny helped pull it off. It was unseasonably warm for late fall. I shivered anyway.

The doctor reappeared with a black bag. At his first touch, I withdrew, just like with Granger. I couldn't help it. Every time anyone or anything touched me there, something yanked me back. He was not surprised and spoke to comfort me.

"Oh, Be-lee. I am all about new arms and new legs, new feet and new hands. An arm to make you a whole boy again, no? An arm to make you very, very normal! Now please, don't be holding back from the doctor. Let the doctor see!"

I forced myself to relax, and he examined my shoulder. He pushed his fingers firmly against the scar tissue until he found the flatness on one bone, the tip of another one. He inspected my ribs and my collarbone on the right side. Then he checked all the same places on my good side.

"Does any of this hurt, my child?"

"No," I said. The only pain being that of shame and longing.

"Such good news," he said to Sunny. "I can help your son—sorry—nephew. Definitely yes! It will not be a functional prosthetic, of course. Purely cosmetic. But these things can help with self-esteem. With psychological healing."

Sunny sighed and mumbled something under her breath. Please God, not a slur.

"Yes, Mrs. Bay-torp?" Dr. Mallick inquired, trying to be polite, thinking she had said something meant to be heard.

"It's Bastrop."

"Of course. My apologies." Vijay smiled and bowed. She snarled. Pursed her lips. I thought she might spit into his gleaming hair as he bowed. I closed my eyes, scared. So close, so close.

The receptionist entered with a saucer in her outstretched hand.

"Please, Mrs. Bar-stroop. If you please, no smoking."

Sunny moaned and slammed her cigarette into it. "Worse than a GD church around here."

"Veda," Dr. Mallick said to the receptionist, "perhaps our guests would like something to drink?" He made a mock drinking motion.

"Do you have Cokes?" I asked. Veda nodded, then turned to Sunny.

"And for the lady?" she asked sweetly.

Sunny said nothing at first, still eyeing that last, half-smoked Camel Veda had confiscated from her.

"Ah'll have some ahs tee, if you got it," Sunny said.

Veda's eyes widened and she blinked rapidly at Sunny, then at Mallick. The doctor and Veda moved to the door, their voices low and quiet. He handed her some cash. Not three minutes later, I saw Veda pass by the window, headed into Lester's Mustang Lounge, money in hand.

"Be-lee, now we must take some X-rays," Dr. Mallick said, drawing my attention back to him. "Have you had X-rays before?"

"No, sir."

"Well then, it is nothing to pain you. We take pictures of your bones, that is all. This way please."

I sat motionless on the X-ray table, as instructed, and stared out the window. Veda passed by, headed back from Lester's Mustang Lounge with our drinks.

I waited for the giant insect-looking machine to pulse, or stream some lights, or at least hum into my shoulder. Nothing. And before the machine could make a peep, Sunny crashed through the door, holding what appeared to be, incredibly, a small bottle of champagne.

"Git off that table, Billy. We're going home."

Here it was, the crash-and-burn I'd feared all morning. My face warped into an airless, tearless cry at first, then went full motor. A runaway, stuttering wail.

Sunny pulled me from beneath the X-ray machine with one hand and flung the little bottle of champagne on the table with the other. Between drooling sobs, I saw the label. It read: *Asti Spumante*.

"Communiss spy bastards!" Sunny dragged me down the hall toward the front door. Dr. Mallick was on our heels, trying one more time to reason with her.

"A terrible mistake on our part, Mrs. Bat-soup. Of course, of course! Your religion forbids alcohol. How could we know? We thought it was what you wanted. A thousand—no—a *million* apologies!"

Veda was near tears, still holding my bottle of Coke.

"But the boy! He is so disappointed," the doctor implored. "Let us give the boy an arm today. He is so sad. Please, we meant no insult. An unfortunate misunderstanding."

"Goddamn heathens! Ahs tee. TEEEE! Don't y'all know plain English?"

"Please, Sunny," I stammered, and dropped to the floor, wrapping myself around a leg of Veda's desk. "Please," I begged. I knew there was only one chance at this. We'd never come back if we left.

She said nothing, just looked down at me disgustedly, mouth agape that I would betray her with these strangers. Then she dug through her massive patent-leather purse, scratching and pawing until she found a previously lost, stale Camel, bent almost at a right angle.

"Hell. Ah'll be in the car." She raised the aged cigarette overhead like an extended middle finger to the world, and rolled out the front door.

After the X-rays, they moved me back to exam room three for the actual fitting, where I sat alone awhile, wrapped in an elephant-patterned blanket and listening to violin music on the radio, and then the news, talking about a parade for the president later that morning.

When the door opened, it was Veda flowing into the room, cradling my new arm against her bosom, as she would cradle a newborn. Veda, beautiful Veda, my angel of restoration, delivering another unforgettable moment for me—rare and precious—the moment of the second chance. I ogled the arm. I ogled her, too, trying to breathe in her perfume without her noticing.

"Go ahead," she said. "Touch it. Hold it. Get familiar." She placed it gently in my lap.

My first thought was, it feels like a log. Close your eyes and it's a log. Open your eyes and it's a hard plastic log covered in weirdly pinkish, spongy rubber "skin."

Dr. Mallick arrived to do the actual fitting, carrying an octopus contraption of straps, buckles, and brass buttons that snapped everything into place. He looped one canvas belt around the upper part of my chest, did some adjusting and tugging, then positioned two other straps across the collarbone and around my neck. With each step of the process to attach it to my body, the arm lost more and more luster in my eyes. Sunny will shit, I thought, when she sees how complicated this is.

It was much heavier than I imagined, hot, totally useless, and had to be worn over a T-shirt to keep from chafing my skin. Although my outer shirt was supposed to hide the straps, one strap always showed in front unless I buttoned my shirt all the way up. Which choked. Not to mention making me look more freakish. What a letdown. All the angst and struggle of the morning for this unwieldy thing? No way it would impress anybody, and would be of no help luring my daddy back. It seemed all we'd managed to accomplish was to put lipstick on my pig of a problem.

Veda managed to cajole Sunny back into the building to pay the bill, and while Sunny paid Veda, I walked over to get a closer look at a tall bronze statue in the lobby. A dancing Indian man with four arms. He stood in a circle that looped from beneath his feet up and over his head, around all his outstretched arms. The man held a small drum in one of his four hands, a flame in another. I'd seen a picture of this guy somewhere before. He gets *four* arms. I get one. Shit.

Sunny went to the bathroom, and I examined the statue's metallic hair. It held a skull and a moon. I swept my finger over the moon, then let it slide toward the skull, enthralled. Veda came up close behind me.

"That is Shiva," she said, her breath tickling my neck. "He is Lord of the Dance."

"More like Lord of the Arms," I said. Veda smiled and touched me lightly on my good shoulder.

"See, Shiva's dance is the dance of all things, the very motion of the universe. He dances inside the circle. This shows that *beginning* and *end* have no meaning. Something ends, another begins. Death becomes life and life becomes death, over and over."

I really wanted to hug her—she had been so kind—but I knew better. Instead, I blurted out something I'd never told anyone, especially Sunny.

"I can feel it, you know. I can still feel my arm sometimes, just like nothing happened. It hurts, it burns. It even itches. In the dark, before I fall asleep, I'd swear it's back." I stared at the floor, embarrassed at what I'd just confessed, afraid she would think less of me. Afraid she'd think I was crazy.

"Sweet boy," she said, bending down, bringing her face close to mine. "People often feel things that cannot be seen."

Veda stood so close, soft-eyed and smiling. A warmth wafting from her to me. A connection. I could see us married one day. Owning a coconut farm. Riding elephants at sunset.

"C'mon Billy. Time to git the hell outta Dallas!" Sunny said as she emerged amid flushing noises from the bathroom, shattering my trance.

On my way out, Veda stopped me at the door and slipped a small cloth Shiva into my shirt pocket. It was as beautiful as she was. Hand sewn in gold, red, black, and blue silk. "For good luck," she said.

I lied to Sunny and told her I was sleepy so she would let me sit in the back seat on our long drive home. While she searched for Stemmons Freeway, making a wrong turn every other block, I took Shiva from my pocket. I propped my fake arm across one leg, and wedged Shiva between a couple of fingers on my new plastic hand, so I could stroke all four silken arms and name each one: Arm of The Dance, Arm of the Moon, Arm of the Skull, Arm of Asti Spumante.

We were cruising south on Stemmons, searching for I-30 when we heard the sirens. The wave of noise came toward us, northbound. Sunny slowed, and a half-dozen police motorcycles screamed past, escorting a motorcade of large, dark convertible limos. Except for the drivers, everybody was hunkered down. In one car, a man in a suit—his necktie flapping in the wind—lay across people cowered in the back. A human shield.

We had no idea what we'd seen, the whole stream of vehicles flashing by in a long black blur. Soon after, at a Dairy Queen in Mesquite, we

heard. Somebody had killed President Kennedy. Sunny, Shiva, and I had
passed through the tail of his surging comet.

We set our corn dogs aside and Sunny led a prayer for his soul, asking
that it be taken directly into the heart of Jesus. As we drove home, there
were more radio reports of the assassination. I took Shiva from my pocket.
I touched the skull. I traced my finger around from top to bottom, bottom to top, hoping Veda was right about the circle.

*   *   *

Three days later, on my ninth birthday, we watched JFK's funeral on television. Well, I watched. Sunny lapsed into a fit of wet, flappy snores on
the couch. There was a half-eaten cake on the coffee table, and alongside
the cake, my new arm. Red gift bow attached.

Even to a nine-year-old, the images were overpowering: flag-draped
coffin, rolling caisson, riderless black horse. Flames on a grave. John Jr.'s
heartbreaking salute.

I too will salute my father, I vowed. If I ever see him again.

*   *   *

I grew older and taller, collecting more arms along the way to match my
size. But I gave them up. They were denials. Euphemisms. Like seating
mannequins around a dining table and calling them Mama and Lucy
and Daddy. You can do it, but it's not Thanksgiving.

Sometimes at night, after my wife and kids go to bed, I sit at the kitchen
table, scotch in hand. I sit in the kitchen because that's where the back
door is, the place family arrives. My ghost arm burns, and I feel all the
parts of me that cannot be seen. I sip the whiskey and sit by the door.
Just in case.

Sex, Lies, and Molokai

SEX MAKES a feeble shield against death. I'd read enough Philip Roth to have known that by now. But some knowledge is hard won, even at my age. I'm sixty-nine.

My Rothian lesson began where many good lessons begin: in a bar. A place called "The FAssT Monkey." It sits right on the harbor at Kaunakakai, Molokai. You can't miss it.

Sal Benito, the owner, originally named it the "Ass Monkey," but the Kaunakakai city council made him change the name, so he painted a sloppy "F" at the front of the Ass, and a "T" at the end, to salvage the twelve hundred bucks he'd spent on the sign.

It's not what you think. Sal wasn't trying to imply anything illicit about his new business. For twenty-seven Chicago winters, he told his wife he wanted to move to Hawaii and open a bar. "When monkeys fly out my ass," she'd said. The monkeys never flew, but Mrs. Benito did try to beat a train across the tracks on her way home from work one afternoon, and lost. Not a fast enough monkey. The man's a genius. Two ironies in one sign.

The FAssT Monkey is where I first met Timina and her German boyfriend, Max. I was looking for carpenters, and the two of them were finishing a covered deck across the front of the bar. Sal introduced us. He knew I wanted to add a couple of bedrooms to my little bungalow out on the western coast of the island.

"You gotta meet these kids," Sal said. "In their early thirties, I'd say. Super nice. Hard workers. And they do excellent work. I give you Exhibit A." He motioned grandly with both arms at his new deck, where we sat with Mai Tais awaiting the couple's arrival.

"Oh, one more thing," Sal leaned over to within a few inches of my face, taking a low, reverent tone. "Listen carefully to me, Mr. Nick Lambert. You simply will not believe your eyes when you see the lady carpenter."

I raised both eyebrows and adjusted the umbrella in my drink.

"Seriously, man. Gird your loins," he said.

He was right. When Timina came in, a step or two ahead of Max, I had that thing happen that happens only once in your lifetime, twice if you're favored—or perhaps cursed—by the gods. The hammer strike to the chest. Throat seized in a gasp. Your whole being filled with the lush opiate of hope and the ridiculous notion that once you meet, neither of you will be able to resist the other. The very feeling I had almost fifty years ago when I first met Bella, my late wife.

As Timina glided toward us, I told myself she wasn't real. There are no real people who look like that. They exist only in movies or slick magazines, a product of camera bullshit and digital tricks.

The hammer pounded and the hammer is your warning. Pay attention to it. It's telling you your brain is surrendering to your dick, and the two of them working together will fuck you up.

*   *   *

The first day Max and I went to work at Mr. Lambert's oceanfront house, and I saw the Basquiat hanging on his living room wall, I knew we had to take it. But Max needed convincing.

"This art theft plan of yours, does it in any way involve you fucking the old goat?" Max asked, handing me our tent poles. Mr. Lambert had invited us to camp next to his pool cabana during construction—where there was a small changing room, toilet, and shower—rather than travel back and forth to Oahu, where we told him we lived. We didn't live there anymore. We didn't live anywhere.

"No way, Maxie." I laughed. "Please tell me you're not jealous of *that* guy."

"He practically drools on you every time you get within arm's length."

"Well, the plan might call for me to get . . . let us say . . . cozy."

"But to be perfectly clear, no sex?"

Shrugging, I said, "What are you calling sex?" I grinned and massaged his shoulders. "Maybe a little nudity. Definitely no penetration. Anywhere."

Max scolded me with his eyes. "Jesus. I've never seen you lust after money like this. You told me you were, how do you say it? A half-and-half Marxist."

"Half-ass," I corrected him. "And this isn't just any money. This is once-in-a-lifetime fuck-you money. This is you-are-now-forever-free money."

Max, deep in thought, jaw cocked, blinked his blue gemstone eyes. Worry broke out across his face. He was a sweet guy, a big statue-of-David sweet guy, but not a natural risk taker. I'd have to coax him along, pull him a little further out of his shell until he realized the potential in it. The beauty. The same as I'd done with rock climbing and base jumping. He was probably imagining all the ways swiping the Basquiat could go south, like a couple of our previous plans. Moving to Hawaii, for example.

"Do you know what we could do with that kind of money? Go back to Kenya and build more schools. God, I could go back to Idaho, back to the rez, and build my grandparents a real house. Build all the tribe's elders real houses of wood and stone. Decent places. Get them out of those shitty tin-can trailers."

"What kind of prisons do they have in Hawaii?" Max asked. I rolled my eyes.

"Lovely ones. With coconut bras and luaus. Now help me stake the tent down. I bet it gets windy out here at night."

The tent finished, we relaxed in oversized, cushy lounge chairs around the quartz firepit, working out the finer details of how to get the Basquiat from Molokai over to Oahu, into Johnny Ono's hands.

"Ono can sell it to the Yakuza for us," I said. "It'll be in Russia or China before we can open our peanuts on a flight to Seattle."

"Dear Timi. Crazy, insane girl," Max said. "I'm beginning to understand that song better and better."

"What song?"

"'American Woman.'"

I winked at him. "Now you're talking."

As I pitched each step of my plan, I took clues from Max's face as it morphed in the dim, swaying firelight. Agreement here. Objection there. I had to drag him along bit by bit, and it took until well after midnight, but I finally had him all in.

We were talked out, and kicked back to soak in the beauty of the place. Nothing but sky and stars and ocean. God it was quiet. No other houses around. Almost never a passing car. Nothing on the ear but the muffled roar of the Pacific looming in the dark.

I took my top off and nudged Max with my foot.

"Come over here," I said.

*   *   *

I got up to pee for the second time that night and saw the carpenters near the pool, out on the lanai, naked in full moonlight. Timina with her hands all over him. Good Lord, it was 3:00 a.m. I slapped water on my face and went back for a second look, to make sure it wasn't yet another weird Ambien vision. No, they were really there. A free, live sex show right at the end of my pool.

Max dropped to his knees and worked his lips up her thigh to the motherland. My erection burst up demandingly, hungrily. And it was no serviceable, you're-late-in-your-sixth-decade boner, but a seventeen-year-old's raging badass hard. A diamond-cutting renegade more than willing to shoot first and ask questions later.

I picked my way through the dark house as if sidestepping land mines, then cat-crept out the back, crouching behind a long row of tall hibiscus bushes, easing a foot or two forward, then pausing. Moving again. Closer. She was sucking his nipples and working the rod.

My erection—a sudden storm that required naming; I called it Eric— had taken me hostage and was refusing to talk to the authorities. I followed Eric toward the pair, and we found a perfect spot in the brush. Far enough away for concealment, but close enough for a full silver-lit view of the action. Timina had Max on his back in the grass. She mounted him, rolling her hips methodically, gently pulling his head forward, to within tongue's length of her breasts.

Eric screamed and strained, threatening to rip through skin. So, I did the only thing a man could do given the circumstance. I beat off like a pubescent monkey and collapsed on my back beneath a canopy of blooming hibiscus and starlight.

I dreamt for hours. But not of Timina. Of Bella.

*   *   *

I met Bella in a barber shop when I was twenty-five and she was almost thirty. She walked me to her chair and draped me in her barber's cloth, and when her fingers traced across my neck, the hammer pounded. The mirror showed us locking eyes, and the hammer pounded so hard it reverberated for thirty years.

I couldn't believe she was standing right there behind me, touching me. Bella—long before I ever laid eyes on her, or knew her name—was basically who I'd sketched on my schoolbook covers as an adolescent.

Drew her in every art class and on every fast food napkin. Doodled her out on church programs during long, boring sermons. She was Sophia Loren fused with Gina Lollobrigida with a heavy dusting of Natalie Wood. Smart and sophisticated. Classic but playful beauty, dripping in sex. Lots and lots of sex. An impossible Lamborghini of a woman. An impossible frankengirl who could have only been constructed by the most naïve teenage boy you could find in Quanah, Washington, population 3,348.

I paid for my haircut and awkwardly peered into her dark gleaming eyes, and while I don't know what she thought of me at that moment, I thought yes, it's you. Her eyes gave the answer. Her eyes said *here*, here is where you belong. Here is your home: look deeply and see your life from this moment to the end, laid out before you. All you have to do is walk in and live it.

We were married for thirty years. Two kids and three grandchildren. She was the best human being I ever met. Keen mind, deep heart, sterling character. She was my best friend and through many hard times, my *only* friend.

She sure didn't deserve the way things ended.

*　*　*

During lunch breaks, Mr. Lambert served us food and drink on the lanai. Max typically took a quick bite or two before going out past the pool to do tai chi, facing the ocean. This fit perfectly with my plan, because it gave me some alone time with Mr. Lambert almost every day.

"Timina," he said. "Beautiful name. And so unusual. I've never heard it." I think he was doing his best to look me in the face, but it was clear he was struggling to keep his eyes from roaming all over me.

"It's Nez Perce. Means *heart* in English."

"From Washington State?"

"Idaho. Grew up on the Selway Reservation."

"We're neighbors!" he said. "I'm from north-central Washington. Not all that far away. I was hoping we'd find something in common."

"More than you know," I said. "Saw all your poetry books. I think we must both love poetry." I despised poetry and my raging high school English teacher, Mr. Bitch.

"Follow me then," he said and motioned toward the house. I unclipped my shorty overalls and let them drop away from the sports bra and yoga pants underneath. He seemed dazed for a moment, averting his eyes down and away. I could have gone around, but I squeezed between him and the table. There was a subtle movement of his head as I brushed by. I think he tried to sniff my hair.

Inside, he explained how the books were organized on shelves along almost every wall except the long, tall wall in the living area, where the Basquiat and another piece hung. He had taken the art down during construction and leaned the canvases against the wall, each covered with a heavy drop cloth.

"See, each bookcase represents a time period—like this one, the nineteenth century. Then within time period, the movements. Here are the nineteenth-century Fireside poets. You know, Longfellow, Whittier, Lowell. All those long-winded guys."

"I'm not well educated on it. I just love it. The reservation schools were pretty bad. And I quit after eighth grade." Utter crap. In fact, I had a BA in Art History from Idaho State.

"But I've always wanted to learn more," I said. Mr. Lambert stood a couple of inches taller. And glowed.

"You're welcome to borrow anything I have. Your own little private library."

"What are these," I asked, picking up two chapbooks with his name on them: Nickolas O. Lambert. "Oh, do you write?" I'd made special note of them a day or two before. My mother always said the best way to butter somebody up is with their own butter.

"Those are distilled vanity," he said.

"But still published."

"By obscure and now defunct little presses. Long out of print. Indiana Jones couldn't find one of them."

"You're being shy," I said, and touched him lightly on his shoulder, my fingers lingering a beat longer than necessary. "I bet they're great. I'd love to read them. Or better yet, you can read them to me."

"To you and Max?"

"Oh God no. Max hates poetry. Just you and me."

* * *

I went to the FAssT Monkey to counsel with Sal.

"You think you might have a chance with Timina? And just so we're straight—in *this* universe, right?" He was still heaving from a near laugh-ter-induced seizure, after hearing my story of Eric in the hibiscus.

"OK, wow." Sal dabbed leftover tears from his face with a bar napkin. "I'm going to surprise you and say, *Why the hell not*? I mean, go for it, man. Follow whatever breadcrumbs she's dropping. You got nothing to lose but a delay in construction because she gets pissed and quits—or more likely, Max crushes your skull with a hammer. You've lived a great life. You're near the end anyway. Go out with a bang. Literally!" Sal looked a little too self-satisfied with his joke.

"Besides, there's plenty of examples of big age differences. That *American Idol* singer, McFee, and her producer husband. Captain Picard from Star

Trek and his woman. Don McLean and wife. Dick Van Dyke has a young honey for chrissake."

"You know what happens when I look in the mirror?" I said. "You remember *Raiders of the Lost Ark*? When the fog or smoke or whatever it is comes out of the ark and melts faces? That's how I feel."

Sal handed me a drink, his most recent attempt at creating a signature cocktail for the Monkey. He wanted me to name it. Something salacious, he'd said.

"The fog got me. Years and years of it. Time accumulated and unleashed. I'm melting. But not mercifully fast, like in the movie. But so very goddamn sloooow. Such a diabolical concept—Nature making you watch your own disintegration."

"Let me stop you there before your morosity runs all my customers off. So—your face ain't what it used to be. Join the club. But look at the rest of you. You're in great shape. You swim, what, couple of miles a day in that fancy lap pool of yours? I've seen you out running up and down hills around the island. You're not paunchy like me. You're not short and bald like me. Hell, I'm ten years younger than you, but that's not buying me anything with the ladies. Enjoy your Richard-damn-Gere self while I'm stuck over here inside Danny-friggin-DeVito."

I took a sip of the unnamed cocktail and cringed. Vodka, Red Bull, and Absinthe.

"Face it, Nick. Just God's way of balancing things out. He gives young men good hair and hard bodies and foolish optimism. He gives old men money and power and regret. Speaking of God, have you told her you're richer than the Big Guy? That might help."

"Ha. Now *that's* an exaggeration. But I did tell her my Basquiat is genuine."

"That fake piece of crap you got in Hong Kong? Jeez. What'd you pay for that?"

"Five hundred bucks. And it's not a fake, it's a *replica.*"

"Nick, Nick, Nick." Sal shook his head slowly. "You do got it bad. Lying outright like that."

"Well, she almost swooned the first time she saw it. Besides, I'm not trying to sell it to her or anything. If she's impressed, then what's the harm? Could help my chances a little."

Sal scratched his bald noggin and looked at me a little too judgmentally.

"Eric," I said.

"What?"

"The drink. Call it Eric. *Eric-in-the-Bush.*"

Sal bulged his eyeballs and jotted it down. "Add a cherry," he said to himself and smirked.

*   *   *

As Sal tells it, he and I met a couple of times back in Chicago. I was a partner at Titus/Crowe/Lambert, an international management consulting firm headquartered downtown in the Hancock Tower. Sal was a financial analyst at my top client, Pexicom Foods, and he was in the audience, he says, during a series of presentations on rebranding I gave to various project teams at Pexicom.

I don't remember Sal from back then because he was just another corporate underling I needed to dazzle with my sparkly PowerPoint and well-honed bullshit. Another hand to shake on the way in and out of a conference room.

But Sal remembers me alright. No one in my last presentation at Pexicom would likely ever forget me. The same way you don't forget the moron who moons your grandmother's funeral procession, or the scary clown hired for your twelfth birthday party who shows up drunk and tries to dry hump your mom.

On that day twelve years ago, the day that burned me permanently into Pexicom's corporate lore and legend, I sat alone in the fifty-second-floor conference room waiting for my audience to arrive. My cell rang. It was Charlie, my brother. We hadn't talked in almost a year. Odd, calling me in the middle of a work day.

"Sorry, Nick. I wish this was a happy call. But it's not. Some backpackers found Dad's remains. In the woods a bit south of the Canadian border. Not far from where the two of you passed through, you know, that time you left the country."

"And they're sure it's him?"

"No mistaking it. A perfect DNA match."

Dazed and numbed, I hung up and stared out the window, mesmerized by Lake Michigan, back turned to the door, oblivious to the shuffle and chatter of a dozen people gathering around the huge glass table behind me.

My mind burrowed back to 1969, the last time I was with my father, the two of us descending steep scree to pitch our tent next to a little mountain lake just this side of Canada. He and I had backpacked four days through the North Cascades wilderness to one of the most remote stretches of the US-Canadian border. I was a month out of high school. We hiked to the border for me to secretly cross over. To escape being drafted into the Vietnam war.

Our trip was glorious. We hiked through pristine forests, up remote trails and over saddle passes between mountains only a handful of people ever get to see. We plucked cutthroat trout and char from crystalline valley streams and camped in the shadow of glaciers. A last father-son hurrah before a likely long separation.

On our last night together, I asked him if the US would win in Vietnam.

"No one wins a war," he said. "One side just comes out less dead than the other."

The next morning as we were about to break camp, Dad caught a leg in some driftwood by the lake and twisted his knee. He was limping pretty badly.

"Dad, let's call this off for now. I'll go later."

"No. I'm fine. I have trouble with this knee sometimes. Loose cartilage. I just need to rest it awhile. It always comes back around."

"We're only two miles from the border," I said. "Come across with me and we'll get it taken care of. We could call Mom and Charlie to drive up and get you."

"Too complicated. If you get caught by the Kanucks, they might look the other way with the war and all. They know American boys are sneaking in illegally. But I'm a different matter. They'd have to do something with me, and I'm afraid that would screw you up somehow."

I helped him back to the tent, and he plopped down on a boulder.

"Now, make me some coffee, then hoof it to The Great White North."

"Let's hike back to the car together," I argued. "What if it gets worse?"

"Hell no! You've come this far. Finish it! I'll stay here and rest the knee an extra day before I pack out home. Do some more fishing."

I left him alone there because he knew what was best and I didn't know much of anything. Because I was a kid and he was a man. Because I didn't have the courage to buck him, to insist, to do something right and smart in the face of stubbornness. I left him because it was the most convenient thing to do. But most of all, I left him because that's what I do, what I'm best at. Leaving problems behind.

As the trail north swallowed me, I turned to see him holding his fly rod overhead in a final farewell.

That was the last time anyone saw him.

The lights of the conference room dimmed, and the Pexicom audience murmured. It was time for me to begin the presentation, but I wasn't present; I'd been pulled out of time and place by Charlie's call and had not yet returned from that trek with Dad. In many ways, I would never return.

Somebody coughed. Somebody called my name. I turned around, but the conference room had vanished—morphed into a mountain campsite. To my eyes, the span of the fancy glass table was now the turquoise surface of an alpine lake. I was again with Dad in the mountains, skipping rocks on a perfect lake, the last thing we did together before he wrenched his knee and I hiked off and left him alone. One more skip. I just needed one more skip.

The projector's remote control flew from my hand and bounced down the long table—skimming the irresistible water of memory—before the goddamn thing shattered and almost blinded their CEO.

*   *   *

We could have stolen the painting and been gone by now, but I was enjoying our stay at Mr. Lambert's place a bit too much, with the ocean and killer view from our campsite. Honestly, I enjoyed all the attention he gave me, and my power to rev the old dude's engine.

Nick—he insisted I start calling him "Nick"—fell into a habit of handpicking several poems for me and delivering them to our tent about dusk each night. He'd also bring Max a cigar, like a consolation prize. It was an expensive cigar, but still.

Max wasn't blind and I could see him growing more anxious, or maybe more secretly jealous by the day, even though he'd agreed to my flirtatious tactics. Could be he sensed a true connection taking root between Lambert and me. Yeah, that surprised me too. Nick Lambert was a decent man. Much better than I first imagined. Brainy with a caring heart. And probably rich as fuck. He was making it hard for me to dislike him.

Max had a laugh about the poetry at first.

"Homework?" he scoffed.

"Don't laugh. These poems are really cool. Mind-bending," I told him. I tried reading him Yeats' "The Second Coming." Four lines in, he waved me off.

"Isn't this more of the kind of horseshit you like to rant about?"

"What can I say? Nick is opening my eyes." I had a pang of regret about blowing off English in high school and college. If only Mr. Bitch or my college English teachers hadn't been such boring douches.

Nick and I sat by the pool each day during lunch break, discussing my previous night's readings.

"I love this one," I told Nick. "Suzanne," by Leonard Cohen. I wasn't faking him. I really did like it.

"So much fun to read. So melodic," I said.

"Cohen recorded it as a song too, but I prefer to think of it as poetry," Nick said.

"Touching a perfect body with his mind," I said. "Beautiful!"

Max had no problem touching me with his body. And yes, that was good. Very good. But his mind? Not so much. I think Max realized our spark was waning—and had been for a while. He was fun, but most likely temporary for me. Once we got the art money from Johnny Ono, I'd have to make a decision. I kind of already knew what that decision would be.

*   *   *

"You call him 'Nick' now? What happened to Mr. Lambert?" Max asked, his neck a little flushed, redness creeping up his jaw.

"Part of the cozy-up process," I said.

"Are we even still taking that ridiculous Basket?" Max asked. "The thing looks like it was painted by his enklekinder, for godsake. Or are we stealing the fucking poetry books instead?"

"It's *Bass-quaaah*. And yes, we are most certainly taking it."

"Then what are we waiting for? I'm anxious to get it done and get away from here. I'm tired of watching him fawn over you."

"I'll lay the bait tomorrow at lunch," I said. "If he bites, then all systems are *go* for tomorrow night."

"Sehr gut," Max said. His mood brightened noticeably, and he kissed me on the forehead. Then the lips. The neck . . .

"I'm beat," I said, gingerly lifting his head off my chest. "Let's save our energy for the big day tomorrow."

*   *   *

Timina pressed me into reading my poetry to her, although it didn't take much pressing. Max was tearing through lumber with a vengeance using his table saw right by the pool. We left our usual outdoor lunch spot and moved inside to escape the noise.

She sat on the couch with me, only one cushion over, and ate a slice of mango as I read the first piece. Halfway through, I looked up from the page at her. She sat with head back and eyes closed. Deep focus on my erudite words? Or lunchtime nap? A rivulet of mango juice slid down the curve of her throat and pooled on the edge of stunning cleavage. By the last line, Eric had arrived. Lick the juice off, Eric shouted. Lick it right goddamn now or I will.

"Maybe you need to get back to work," I said, trying to hint Timina out of the house and tamp Eric down. We'd been out of Max's line of sight too long.

"I've got time for another," she said. "Mango?" She scooted my way and held a slice to my lips.

"I'll read another one tomorrow at lunch. Let's make them last."

"OK, tomorrow. It's a date. Can I use your bathroom?" She said *date!* Eric yelled. Did you hear that? *Date.*

Timina stood and headed toward the bath, then stopped.

"How about doing it tonight? Max is flying to Oahu after we finish the framing today. He's not coming back till late tomorrow."

"Sure," I said. Holy shit. Is this actually happening?

"I haven't seen your little beach," she said. "You know, below the cliff. I noticed there's a trail leading down there. I could make us some sandwiches and drinks to take along."

"A poetry picnic," I said.

"About dusk then? I can't wait to see the sunset from that spot."

"I'll go down early. Build a fire."

Oh, we gonna build a fire alright.

Shut up, Eric.

* * *

In Nick's bathroom, I rummaged around until I found his Ambien, a key part of the plan. I dumped about five of them in my pocket. Enough to do the job, but not enough to be noticed as missing. And not enough to kill anybody, I hoped. My job was to lure him down the trail to that beach and Cosby his drink. Do whatever else I could think of to keep him down there.

Max would pretend to leave by driving off in our truck, then double back after dark. His job was to take the painting from its frame, cut the canvas from the stretcher, roll it up, and tube it. After which he'd reassemble the empty frame and stretcher and put it back under the drop cloth, and all would appear as before.

I'd meet Max back at the bungalow, and we'd drive to the airport while Nick slept it off on the beach. Johnny Ono had chartered a private puddle-jumper to hop us over to Honolulu. We'd give the Basquiat to Ono there, then fly to the mainland where it'd be much easier to hide and wait for our bitcoin payment.

When Nick woke, he'd stumble home, wondering WTF? Hours later he might think to look under the drop cloth. Then? File an insurance claim, get a fat check, buy another bougie trinket. Rich people never really lose money.

No harm, no foul.

*　　*　　*

For years after my father's disappearance in the North Cascades, rumors circled my family like toxic crows. The gossip and theories hatched easily, given my parents' history of frequent and virulent public fights. Some assumed he took the opportunity to disappear into Canada with me, two deserters for the price of one. Others said Dad hiked back out as planned, left his car at the trailhead as a decoy, and was picked up by an accomplice. Most likely "the other woman"—everyone seemed to have a different idea of who she was—and the two of them shipped off to Alaska.

Finding his bones may have proven them wrong, but gave me no peace. The remains bore signs of predation. Bear? Cougar? There were plenty of both around there. How godawful.

Before Charlie called me with the news that day at Pexicom, I'd spent decades telling myself Dad was alive. Believing he deserted our family was better than knowing what truly happened. Knowing what happened because I left him behind. If I had been with him, he might have lived. Instead, he died alone in the wilderness at the top edge of America saving me from an insane war.

Finding his bones planted seeds of ice in me that grew to crippling proportions. My greatest strength—an ability to focus on a problem or a task, X-ray it and turn it over in my mind until a solution was found—evaporated. But I mastered new skills. Became sensei of apathy. Mack daddy of aloofness.

A great barrier of numbness rose between me and everything I had previously cared about, including Bella and the kids. Client project overdue? Fuck them and their artificial deadlines. Partner meetings? What's left to be said—we're all rich assholes now; go home and drink. Another grandchild on the way? What's the point, really?

As the ice reached glacial volume, I urged Bella to escape the cold with me. I could no longer survive the doubling of winter, with Dad's frozen bones lodged inside me and Chicago gloom pressing in from the outside. Let's move to San Diego, I begged Bella. Or Las Vegas. Florida. Any place without winter.

Bella wouldn't budge. We'd lived in Chicago forever, our entire adult lives built up from the roots laid there.

"How could we possibly move?" she'd said. "Our kids and grandkids are all here. Is long distance love really love?" She wanted all her family within arm's reach, and refused to even talk to me about moving. I wouldn't let it go and pushed and pushed until there was nothing left of our marriage but a smoking, twisted wreck.

I moved alone to San Diego. Tried for months, by long distance, to convince Bella to join me. Finally, I filed for divorce. Maybe she would change her mind, maybe not. Ice cares not about the human heart.

My son Donny called the day Bella received the divorce papers.

"When did you turn into a class-A prick?" he asked.

"Excuse me?"

"Today? Today of all days? Today's the day you hit her with this?"

"First, I have no control over when they serve papers. And second, what's special about today?"

"Her biopsy today, Dad. They confirmed the tumor is malignant."

"Tumor? No. No. God no. She never told me."

"Never said? Or you never heard?"

"I'll take the next flight."

"No. Stay in Cali. Seriously, we don't need you around right now. Marla is so furious, she might hurt you."

I moved to Molokai a month after Bella's funeral, as far from my past as I could get and still be in the United States. Donny calls a couple times a year, but never comes out.

Marla, my daughter, is another matter. She not only refuses to come to Molokai; she refuses to let me visit her family in Indianapolis. Two Christmases ago, I emailed her five first-class tickets. She ignored them and replied with this message:

> *Daddy, you put a continent and the Pacific between us, and now you're sad we don't come to see you? You can't jump out of the fucking boat, and then blame the ocean when you drown.*
> *—Marla*

Now, I'm adding bedrooms to my place. Bait, pure and simple. May be too late to salvage anything with my kids, but I might still have a chance with the grandchildren.

Might.

*   *   *

As dusk approached on the night of my poetry date with Timina, I carried firewood down the steep trail. Technically, it's a public beach—there are no private beaches in Hawaii—but it was so small and remote and unknown, even to most locals, that no one ever went down there. It backed up to a steep cliff and faced the Pacific across a small, partially protected inlet.

The grasses were shoulder high on either side of the trail, and as I stood on the beach looking up, all I could see of Timina descending was the jet-black top of her long hair, her head bobbing in and out of sight.

She popped out of the vegetation and popped my eyes, wearing a white bikini, with a purple sarong coverup around her waist. In the golden-hour light, she was all cocoa skin and hammer firm.

I took her hand to help with the last step down (like she needed help, right?), and in what I meant as a joke about the tall weeds, recited:

> *The woods are lovely, dark and deep,*
> *But I have promises to keep,*
> *And miles to go before I sleep,*
> *And miles to go before I sleep.*

"OMG. Is that one of yours?" she asked.

"Well . . . yes. From way back." I couldn't be sure, but I may have heard Robert Frost banging his coffin lid.

We laid out the blanket, and Timina handed me a cold Yeti cup. "Rum punch," she said.

The drink seemed overly bitter to me. After a polite sip or two, I set mine aside and read her the first few poems I'd brought for the occasion.

Poems I'd actually written. The sun did its slow-motion dive into the ocean and she removed her sunglasses, and we sat in awe of that celestial show that never, never gets old.

Edging toward her, I said:

And the sunlight clasps the earth

And the moonbeams kiss the sea:

What is all this sweet work worth

If you kiss not me?

"Yours again?"

I nodded. Sorry, Shelley.

It was time to take Sal's advice. Give it a shot and kiss her. There would never be a better time or place.

I leaned in. She sat upright, made no attempt to move back. Our lips a micron apart, she put a finger to my mouth, as if to shush me.

"Wait," she said. "You still have your own teeth? Right?"

I kissed her anyway. She held my head in her hands.

She stood. Took a long pull from her Yeti. Dropped the sarong.

"You're not drinking?"

"Sorry, a little too bitter for me."

She unleashed her top and let it fall. I felt my neck flush and the hammer pound.

"I'm going for a dip. Want to come?"

"Go ahead. I'm right behind you." Eric was making it very awkward for me to stand at that precise moment.

A speck of sun turned the lower third of sky a layered, pastel wash. Timina swam along the rocky spit about fifty yards out and vanished. I thought she dove after something. Then her head jerked violently out of the water and plunged back under a second later.

A jolt rushed down my backbone. I jumped up and called to her.

Screamed to her. In the quickening dark, it was impossible to tell exactly where she was or what was happening. All I knew was she didn't answer—probably couldn't answer—and if I had any chance of finding her, it had to be then.

I ran into the rising tide and swam to the last place I'd seen her. No moon yet, only dark sky over dark water. I treaded and hovered until I spotted something a shade darker than sky on the surface. Her head above water. Floating on her back. I got to her. Blood streaming all around.

I hadn't worked as a lifeguard since high school, but it came back in a blink. I got the proper grip on her—she neither moved nor spoke, in shock I suspected—and frog-kicked us back to shore.

Her left leg was gone below the knee, sheared off, and there were deep punctures in her hip and thigh. I lowered her to the blanket and pushed both hands against scraps of muscle and veins and blood—so much blood. I sat motionless for a moment refusing to believe it, tried to scream through a dry, clamped throat, and watched the beach spin around me and the sea and sky vibrate and misalign.

Timina's breathing was too shallow. Her eyes fluttered; her body convulsed. I made a tourniquet of the sarong. I doubled the blanket and wrapped her in it. There was no way I could carry her and run or even walk up the trail, so I left her there and ran the half mile back to my house, to get to the landline, the only way on the western end of Molokai to call in a shark attack.

I burst through the back door of the bungalow and found Max with my stupid, fake Basquiat half rolled up on the kitchen table, a shipping tube propped in a chair.

"Timina! Timina! Down the trail. Run man run! A shark got her. She's on the beach."

"Oh mein Gott! No!"

He flung the canvas on the table and shot out the door. I dialed 911.

For a few hours at the hospital, Max and I took turns convincing each other she would make it. Timina was young and God knows how healthy, how strong. She would make short work of mastering a prosthetic. Max laughed at the fantasy of them base jumping off the Eiffel Tower by Christmas. I thought carefully and decided the next two poets for her should be Whitman and Dickinson. We paced and drank bad coffee and told each other more and more lies.

Near daybreak, the doctors told us they'd lost her.

* * *

All I can think to do is run. I run east, coaxing painful speed from my aged, rotting knees. Run east, hoping the morning will be merciful and my heart will explode or my brain seize. Run east, to my favorite spot, the overlook above the Kalaupapa Peninsula, where Father Damien cared for the lepers. Where his reward was leprosy. Here, I'm spent. Throw my shirt in a tree and flop on my back and pound fine red dirt into my sweat-soaked chest. Yeah, pound dirt into my skin as penance for the reckless delusion I could ever escape the ice—even on a tropical island—and turn a young lover into a time machine.

I stand at the cliff top where the rainforest drops two thousand feet and surges down to the Pacific, the land countless shades of green in the nascent dawn. The sun rises, dragging behind it a stream of colors unnamed except, perhaps, in the heart of God. If the bastard has a heart.

No one deserves such beauty. Yet here I am.

What a gorgeous hell.

The Kazminskis

NASH KAZMINSKI had never kidnapped a child before, but how hard could it be? He had two big advantages: he was a janitor at Tucker Elementary in Cragmont, West Virginia, where Evan—the boy he planned to take—was a third grader. And he and Evan were already pals. It would be easy to talk the boy into leaving school with him.

Evan was obsessed with motorcycles—never drew pictures of anything else, the teachers said. Nash planned to ride his new Suzuki to school and use it to lure Evan off the playground. Let the boy ogle the bike and offer him a ride. They'd be halfway to the wilderness zone of Cragmont National Forest before anyone missed the pale little wisp of a boy, the kid in the dirty clothes who rarely smiled and never spoke. Selectively mute, the SPED teachers called it. Fully capable of speech, but silent.

He'd take the boy on a Thursday, during that chaotic time between lunch and the end of mid-day recess. Every Thursday, the aged and slow-footed Mrs. Paxton was on duty, left alone to watch dozens of children zoom across the dusty playground like rolling, intersecting clouds of starlings. Paxton wouldn't notice one less kid, especially not Evan the mute. He was practically invisible.

This was the week to do it. All the food and camping gear were ready, and nothing was going to stop him. But first, he had to say goodbye to his grandfather, Kaz.

* * *

Born Oskar Kazminski eighty years ago in Poland, his American name was "Kaz." To his family in Poland, all those decades ago, he was Misio as a child, and Oskar as he got older. But to the SS at Treblinka, he was known only by the tattoo on his forearm: T-15051.

Under the night sky of Treblinka, during the worst of winter, Oskar Kazminski couldn't picture himself living to daybreak. He didn't have the luxury of imagination. The word *future* was a mocking cruelty. Thinking about tomorrow instead of *right-here-right-now-what-now* meant you were already lost. Only the soft and weak wasted energy on such nonsense. Those people woke up dead.

There were no ovens at Treblinka. Instead, open burning pits consumed the endless stream of corpses. His mother and sisters were last seen as smoke angels near sundown on their first day there, blowing across the gray hellscape of the camp.

The pits demanded wood, and wood had been, so far, Oskar's salvation. Age thirteen and strong enough to work, he was assigned to one of the mule-drawn firewood wagons circling back and forth into the forest for fuel. *Holzjungen,* the guards called them. *Wood boys.* Wagons going out, passing other wagons coming back, all day and all night. He was valuable as holzjungen, and that had so far kept him from the gas chamber. That, and maybe the fact he was not Jewish but Polish Catholic. But Oskar knew. He knew being a goy would only delay, not cancel, his trip into the pits. All Poles—Jews or not—were vermin to the Reich.

Oskar gathered firewood and tried not to think at all. Thinking was for humans, not vermin. The work was hardest at night, tripping and stumbling. Falling, almost too weak from starvation to rise again, looking straight up into the blackness of the treetops, and beyond the trees at a cold ceiling of stars.

His father—before the SS shot him in a ditch outside their village—

said scientists claim the stars are merely orbs of burning gas. But they are wrong, his Tata explained. Stars are the eyes of God, surrounding the world. Always there. Watching and recording. Judging. Ten million omniscient eyes of God.

*　*　*

Nash rode his new Suzuki dirt bike to Kaz's grave and talked to the headstone.

"Don't be mad, Kaz," Nash said. "But I'm taking Evan, the kid I've been telling you about."

The only response he got was the crinkle and thwap of a plastic bag cartwheeled along by hot September wind. It caught in the spokes of his bike and flapped like a snared duck.

"Don't try to talk me out of it. I've got a good plan. It'll work."

Footsteps chomped softly on the wet pea gravel behind him. Two elderly ladies trudged by, wobbly-kneed, carrying Walmart bags brimming with plastic flowers. He paused until they were out of earshot.

"Kaz, you're not going to believe this one, but I think Evan could be my son. He might be your *great*-grandson! I found some forms at school," he said. "On top of the shredder in one of the SPED rooms. Get this: Evan's mother is Jett Brinker-Smith! Jett Brinker!"

Speaking her name aloud to Kaz—*Jett Brinker*—flooded his head with high school graduation night ten years ago. The traditional open party thrown by the Wilkins family at their lake house. Everybody welcome, the flyers said. The only kind of party Nash could go to, one where he didn't need an invitation. The annual Wilkins graduation party was mythological at his school. So much so, he never believed the stories.

Nash had few friends, and none of them were courageous enough to show up at the lake house that night, so he sat alone by a small firepit next to the boat dock, looking back at throngs of people flowing in and out of the house, across the lawn and into the surrounding woods, many stumbling drunk.

It was the usual deal for him—always a spectator and never a participant. Until Jett Brinker made her way to the dock, blouse unbuttoned and flowing behind her like a supervillain's cape. She plopped into his lap.

"Ever kissed a girl, Nasty?" she asked, squinting at him, smelling of weed and Jack. That's what everyone called him, *Nasty*. Nasty-Ass Nash.

"Not . . . really," he said, not sure where to look, her flimsy bra barely containing the spillage.

"Not, not, really." She mocked him and laughed.

"Reallllly not?" She tugged his face toward hers to put them eye to eye—Nash clear-headed and sober, Jett droopy-lidded and not. She laced her fingers around his neck and slid wet lips across his mouth, then tongued him, soft and flickery.

Nash had never been that close to a girl before, but discovered he was a natural at the tongue thing. He also learned very, very quickly that a real gametime erection has little in common with the tamer, practice-at-home kind. In what seemed like one motion she had his zipper down and his beast out and bare to the moon. One firm girl-hand squeeze and three strokes later Nash almost shot her eye out.

"Never before, huh? As I figured," she said. "Take a little rest and don't go nowhere. I gotta collect on a bet and get another drink. Then I'm coming back to fuck you stupid."

* * *

After the war, traversing a thousand miles of rubble and obscenity as a dead-eyed, starving teen, Kaz never thought once of tomorrow. He thought only of pushing his right foot forward, and if that worked, his left. Right, left, right, left across Poland, across Germany before the Soviets closed half of it down. Right, left into France. On to the coast. An American merchant marine ship, the SS *Attucks* leaving Marseilles and bound for North Carolina. He lied about his age in stumbling English and signed on as a galley mate.

Kaz dropped to his knees and cried openly when they showed him the food. He wiped tears as he cut up burlap bags full of potatoes and carrots for stew. Sliced reams of fresh bread. Brewed gallon after gallon of coffee, something he'd never tasted, and served it to the crew with milk and sugar. Milk! Sugar!

After galley duty that first night, he stood near the stern of the *Attucks*—already miles from sight of any land—and scanned the dome of the darkest midnight sky he'd ever seen, darker even than at Treblinka. Kaz pulled an American apple from the filthy duffel at his feet, the bag holding his few possessions.

He turned the apple and watched it catch the silvery glow of the ship's lights. How phenomenal it was—to hold a piece of magic in your hand. Kaz fought tears. What such a thing would have meant in the camp. A week's food. An immense bargaining chip. Something some would have traded their bodies for. Something others would have gleefully killed for.

Overhead hung the ten million eyes, packed thick enough in spots to form a sparkling, misty river across the great black. If they *are* God's eyes, they are the same eyes that watched Joachim, a fellow holzjungen, slip Kaz a human hand one night—furtively retrieved from one of the cremation pits. A meager offering of friendship, something to slow the starvation that dissolved Kaz a little more each day.

Ten million eyes watched him gnaw what he could from the charred bones. They saw him, crushed with shame, drenched in sin and damnation, run and hide from the sky. He embraced his brokenness and slumped in the hollow of an oak, gnashing and ripping at the crusty strands of meat. Just like a scabrous rat in a sewer, he told himself. Vermin after all.

Kaz gazed skyward from the deck of the *Attucks*. How could they be the eyes of God? Watching the world and its peoples consumed by demons. Continents set ablaze. God's children's sacred souls ripped screeching from their flesh and bone. Raped, tortured, and incinerated. Surely, the God Kaz was taught to love could not idly watch the annihilation of His loving children! How could He see such things and not act? Is He blind? Dead?

Or worst of all—and the most unthinkable: does He just not care?

Kaz put the apple back in the bag and took out the striped pants he'd worn at Treblinka, the pants he'd worn for most of his thousand-mile trek across a shattered, smoking land. He dropped them over the side, let the ocean swallow them. Next, the shirt. Finally, he held the cap, free of lice at last, and rolled it in his hands. He peered over the taffrail at an inky Atlantic, calm and smooth as obsidian except for the course the *Attucks* scratched across it.

"No," he said to no one. "This I keep. This I keep as witness to horror. As proof of passage. This I take to America. A reminder. No matter what happens, no matter how hard Oskar Kazminski struggle, how much hardship, how much pain, I look at this and remember. Nothing for the rest of my life—*nothing* will be this bad. I overcome Treblinka, I overcome anything."

Kaz felt an impulse to look at the sky as he made his vow, but caught himself and kept his head down. Best to focus on his earthly journey now—now that maybe he had a future after all—to keep his feet on the ground and his eyes on the horizon. He would never look up again. His disappointment with the stars—those useless eyes— stabbed too deeply into him.

*   *   *

Nash scanned the cemetery to make sure no one could hear and took a clipped newspaper article from his back pocket, from the *Cragmont Weekly Times*, and read aloud to Kaz.

"Says here: Couple Arraigned on Charges of Meth Possession and Child Neglect and Endangering. *Jeremy 'Skeeter' Smith, age 28, and his wife Jett Brinker-Smith, also age 28, were taken into custody and charged with meth-amphetamine possession and intent to traffic, as well as child neglect and endangering. Eagle County Sheriff Dan Clements reports that his deputies are gathering evidence toward a meth manufacturing charge with intent to traffic.*"

He paused to let Kaz absorb this information and stared at moss growing thick in the letters of his grandfather's name, as if trying to erase it.

Nash read on: "*The couple have a minor child, age 9, (name withheld by the* Weekly Times*). Clements said 'evidence suggests the child was severely underfed, and locked in a tool shed to sleep most nights.' The child is currently in the custody of Children's Protective Services.*

"I did the math, Kaz. Evan's birthday is just over nine months from my high school graduation date. There's something I never told you, and I'm ashamed to say it now—but I had relations with Jett that night." Nash wiped hair from his face and locked his fingers behind his neck. Slowly shook his head. *I've been such a disappointment to so many.* And now, even to Kaz.

Although he knew she had fucked him ironically, or to win a bet or prove some point to somebody, he never really stopped thinking about Jett. He felt like an idiot every time he caught himself fantasizing about her in some romantic way. Don't think of her at all, he told himself, especially not in lame, hazy daydreams where you come home from work and the two of you eat popcorn on the couch and watch Netflix, or play in the sprinklers with your dog and your kid. A thousand dollars says she doesn't remember your name. Has no memory of being on that dock with you. Couldn't pick you out of a lineup.

As Nash left the party on graduation night, his last glimpse of Jett was of her and Skeeter Smith in the back of Skeeter's pickup, Skeeter banging her from behind. Nash spotted her only once since, a couple of years before Kaz died, walking into a Walgreens. Somebody told him that soon after graduation, she married that druggy Skeeter Smith and they had a son. Otherwise, she had successfully disappeared into the nearby countryside, absorbed into one of the dense hollers around Cragmont.

"The kid in this article *has* to be Evan!" Nash shouted. He crumpled the paper and hurled it toward his bike, watched it roll against a marble statue of a Civil War soldier, rifle and bayonet at the ready. He dropped his head into his hands and teared up for a moment, thinking about the pointlessness of talking to the guardians of the dead, deaf as they are, the grass and trees and rocks.

Nash didn't tell Kaz about Jett and Skeeter in the pickup. There might have been other boys with Jett that night as well, who knows? He didn't tell Kaz these things because he was convinced Evan was his son. No one else. *His.*

He saw himself in Evan's face, in his walk and his smile—on the rare occasions the kid smiled. Nash saw his mother and Kaz in Evan, in the cut of his brow, the shape of his ears. The way he crinkled his forehead when he bore down on one of his motorcycle sketches.

And Nash was loath to admit it, but he also saw his father, Marek, in Evan. Marek, Kaz's only child, the man Kaz renamed *The Cold Fish* because of his treatment of Nash. That's what most convinced Nash that Evan was his son: seeing a trace of his father in the boy, something he'd never willingly see. If he saw *that*, it must be true. His mind would never play a trick that cruel.

"I've got to take the boy, Kaz. You know that," he said to the grave and the rocks and the trees.

"You know that more than anyone. I've got to take him before the Bright Lady does."

*   *   *

The Bright Lady came to Nash for the first time late on the night of his thirteenth birthday. He looked up from his pillow, dazed and half awake, and thought it was his mother sitting on the edge of the mattress. But the woman was much younger than his mother, much prettier, and her flowing nightgown shone with soft luminescence, as if woven from the stuff of fireflies.

"I'm dreaming," Nash said aloud, catching himself staring at her shapely breasts, fully visible and nicely lit through the sheer, glowing cloth.

"You're not," the woman said.

Nash sat up. His first impulse was to scream, but that would bring his father in, stomping and cussing. He wasn't yet entirely sure it wasn't a dream, and if he woke the whole household over an imaginary, half-naked woman on his bed . . . well, he would move even higher on his father's shit list. Besides, if a dream *begins* with a half-naked woman on your bed, how does it end?

"Who . . . who are you?" he asked.

She scooted closer. Nash looked at her more closely, disarmed by her stunning beauty.

"I need to tell you some things," she said. "These are not easy things, but you need to know. So you can decide." She held both his hands in hers and he felt an entirely new kind of warmth, a trust, an instant alliance. Her soft, honest eyes told him she knew important things about him. Secret things.

"Your father hates you, Nash," The Bright Lady said. "Marek Kazminski can't stand the sight of you."

"I know. It's because I can't do anything right, isn't it?"

"You can never find the right wrench," she said, her voice gentle, musical. "How hard is it to find the right fucking wrench when a man needs one?"

"I get nervous when he sends me after stuff," Nash said. "I'm so afraid of doing the wrong thing, I just mess up."

"What would help a lot would be you pulling your head out of your ass and start acting like a man," she said softly. "You're almost grown now for God's sake."

"I get confused. I forget what I'm supposed to do sometimes. I'm sorry I'm sorry I'm sorry."

"And, you're still pissing the bed," she said. She threw the covers back and ran her hand over the sheets. "Jesus, you've done it again tonight. Who pisses the bed when they're thirteen?" The Bright Lady sighed and shook her head. Showed Nash a pained half smile.

Nash pressed his chin to his chest and heaved quietly, salty tears dripping across his lips.

"No wonder he hates you. Stop sniffling. Are you a titty baby?" The Bright Lady asked in a whisper and pushed his chin up.

"It happens without me even knowing it," Nash shouted. "I just wake up and it's there. It's not on purpose, I swear. It's not on purpose! You believe me, don't you?"

"Only titty babies wet the bed, like your daddy says. Like The Cold

Fish says. That's what Kaz calls your father, isn't it—'The Cold Fish'?"

"And Kaz calls Mom 'The Fish Keeper.' 'Cause she jumps every time Dad says boo. And 'cause she never takes up for me. She's too afraid."

"Nash, if you keep doing this, you'll never have a girlfriend. Or a wife. Nobody wants to sleep with an asshole who pisses the bed."

"I don't know what to do," he said. "I'm sad and confused all the time. *All* the time. I hate it so much when he yells at me."

"Well, I'm here to help you decide. Do you want to live here, knowing your father will always hate you? Will always wish you had never been born? Do you want to live like that?"

"No," Nash said, wiping tears and snot from his face with the tail of his T-shirt.

"Don't you think your parents would be much better off without you?"

"Sure. But where would I go?"

"Come with me. We can escape this place together. We can give The Cold Fish what he wants once and for all. We can make it like you were never born."

*   *   *

Oskar Kazminski never thought of himself as a business owner, but there he was, about to sign papers to buy Tubby's Diner in the little town of Cragmont, West Virginia. It was 1969, twenty-two years after he walked off the *Attucks* into America.

Owning Tubby's made him truly American. He'd been a citizen for years, but owning a business sealed the deal, as Americans liked to say. Everyone in America called him Kaz, the way Americans do, almost from his first step aboard the *Attucks* at age fourteen. He liked it because it was so American, so efficient. Why use five syllables when one will do? Why bother learning a person's name when you can just bestow a more convenient one? Kaz the unlikely, Kaz the survivor. He was proud to get a nickname. You only get a nickname if you are accepted. Beloved, maybe.

He paused a moment before entering the bank to finalize the purchase of Tubby's and looked up at the lush mountains surrounding Cragmont. He could see down the steep incline of First Street all the way to the violent rapids of the Raven River, and two miles further to the iron underpinnings of the double-decker Raven Gorge Bridge that carried cars on the upper roadway, and trains on the lower. He had driven across it into Cragmont just that morning, glimpsing over the edge from time to time at the unsettling view of a thousand-foot drop to the churning river.

It was a day to remember to be sure, the day he finally started believing that tomorrow could exist. A long, beautiful, endless stream of tomorrows.

Here he was in a July place in America with a sky so blue and a world so green it felt like a cartoon, with a cartoon banker handing him a cartoon pen to scratch his Polish name down and own something. So ridiculous. So unreal.

Kaz happily worked brutal hours and the little diner thrived. Soon, he married one of his waitresses—a holler girl named Luleen—and they tried to be happy, but no matter how long he lived in the blue-sky, green-tree cartoon mountain world, Treblinka stalked him. Treblinka's shitty gray specter smothered him in the night. The stench of the cremation pits burned his mouth and throat. He still tasted that hand. That hand! The palm and wrist, the charred fingers. Ashy shadows of his mother and sisters skulked around corners. What right did he have to live in this beautiful dream?

Kaz was no coward. He didn't hide inside golf or booze or women. No meth, no coke, no oxy. His only escape, the only quieting of his mind and soul, was work and more work. He kept Tubby's open twenty-fours. He filled his mind and energy with his business—staff schedules, deliveries, payroll—to the point where there was no room for Treblinka to edge in. But, also no space in him for his boy, Marek.

* * *

The Bright Lady rode on the handlebars of Nash's new birthday bicycle as he pedaled where she directed, down the shoulder of Highway 61 toward the Raven Gorge Bridge. It was three a.m.

Nash leaned the bicycle against the waist-high, flagstone railing of the 1930's bridge. A flat slab of concrete about ten inches wide topped the railing, all the way across the gorge. About mid-bridge, he and The Bright Lady leaned out and looked down, looking into nothing but rich, smooth blackness.

"How far down is it?" Nash asked.

"All the way," she said, and jumped up on the narrow ledge. "Throw the bike over. Let's see how long it takes to hit. You won't be needing it after tonight."

Nash watched her gown lift and twist in the wind, brushing his face, rising and falling around her nakedness.

"Throw that damn piece of Walmart junk over, why don't you? You know it's the cheapest bike they could find."

He grabbed the handlebars with both hands and hung the front tire over the rail.

"Attaboy. Now grab the back."

Nash lifted the back tire and pushed until the chain clanked across the concrete ledge. The wind rose just as he found the bicycle's tipping point. With a quiet whoosh, the bike was swallowed into the night sky.

"You're stronger than you look," The Bright Lady said. "I'm impressed." She bent down to give Nash a hand up on the railing. He scrambled up and stood next to her.

"You ready?" she asked.

Nash stared downriver and saw nothing but darkness stretched across a moonless, starless world. No horizon, no up or down. Nothing.

She took his hand and gave him a beatific smile.

"Let's go find your bike."

"I'm not sure," he said, shifting a foot, swaying. The wind pushed at him, and his gut cinched. He bent his knees and huffed, trying to rebalance. The headlights of a car flicked in the corner of one eye, but he fought off the impulse to turn his head, convinced that even a small shifting of weight would throw him over.

"Of course you're sure! We already covered this. You're worthless. They hate you. Come on!"

The Bright Lady dropped his hand and floated out over the chasm in front of him. She unbuttoned her firefly gown all the way down and let the breeze sail it behind her like the tail of a fiery kite. She reached for him, hovering with open arms, three feet out in space.

"You've come this far. Finish it. Come to me, Nash. Now."

"I'm falling!"

"No! Flying! Let's fly!" She laughed.

Her glow pulsed red, blue, red, and she began to fade, then disappeared completely when Nash heard the voice of Deputy Baskin rise from behind him.

"Son—son," the deputy said, his voice a notch above a whisper. He stood on the bridge deck a foot behind Nash, the two of them backlit by the red-blue strobe of Baskin's emergency lights.

"Son, don't move. I've got you. I'm going to put my arms around your legs. Easy now. Please God don't flinch. Just lean back. Just lean back into me."

*   *   *

Kaz drove to Morgantown to visit his grandson at The Hawthorne House for Teens, the mental facility where Nash was sent for counseling and recovery. It was Nash's second commission to Hawthorne in three years, the first being after Deputy Baskin coaxed him off the Raven Gorge Bridge. And now he was back a second time—nearing the end of a six-week residency—after The Bright Lady returned and convinced him to down half a bottle of his mother's Ambien.

They sat in well-worn oak and leather chairs in the small library, sunlight drilling through half-opened blinds. Kaz sipped heavily sugared coffee and cringed watching Nash gulp Mountain Dew.

"I come here to tell you things," Kaz said. "Things maybe you not know."

"I'm sorry about all this," Nash said, and looked at his feet, his hands, anywhere but into his grandfather's eyes. He sighed and shook his head and kept his face down as Kaz spoke.

"You know you were born at home, right? Not hospital." Nash nodded.

"Your mother was alone. Marek was in mountains. Hunting."

Nash lifted his head and smirked. "Yeah?" he said. "Sounds about right."

"You come early. Two, three weeks. A surprise. Your mama call me. In panic, much pain. She worries the house is so remote. Up steep gravel road. She call ambulance, but they never show. Maybe got lost?"

"Jesus," Nash said. "I never heard that part."

"I drive there fast. Drive Jeep fast up that road. Maybe half mile to house, trees fallen over road. I leave Jeep and run. Run to house."

Kaz saw Nash glance down at his cane, and thought, yes, I need a cane to walk now, and still not very well. It's hard to imagine me back then, running up a gravel road.

"I find your mama on bed. Horrible pain. Not normal pain, no, something wrong. 'Get me to hospital!' She scream at me. Her voice desperate, like trapped animal. Her belly puff up so big. Not look right to me."

"How would you know? You weren't a doctor," Nash said.

"On train from our village to Treblinka. I remember woman in cattle car with us who look very same. My mama—your great-grandmama Krystyna—rub woman's belly. Knew baby turned wrong. Breech. Mama call me over. Show me bulge of baby's head. I watch and Mama gently turn baby, so head is down. 'Oskar, see,' she said. 'If baby not too big, this sometimes work. You might need to know one day,' she said. 'Where we go.'"

"So, you did that to Mom? To me?" Nash asked.

"You are here, right?" Kaz smiled knowingly and tapped his coffee mug against Nash's pop bottle. "Your mama push you out few minutes later. That was best night of my life. Best!"

He remembered more from the night of Nash's birth: While Nash suckled his first meal, Kaz found Marek's chainsaw and walked down the road to cut a path for the ambulance through the fallen trees. As he cut, his thoughts turned back to his mother all those years ago, delivering a doomed child to a doomed woman onboard a death train. Was that an act of great hope? Or insanity? He smiled at the memory of it—turns out she *did* save two lives that night, just not the two in that cattle car.

Kaz killed the chainsaw and sat on a log in the dark and the quiet, waiting for the EMTs. Despite himself, he looked at the stars for the first time since crossing the Atlantic, into a sky massively freckled with light, and he still didn't know if he was looking at globes of hellfire or portals to the mystic. All he knew was that some new joy had come to Earth that night.

Come to him. A new potential. On that night, at least, he was willing to look heavenward again, and contemplate.

Their visit done, Nash and Kaz walked down the front drive of Hawthorne House to Kaz's pickup. Nash sat on the tailgate. The old man stared at his grandson, his American-July-blue-sky grandson, and felt overwhelming shame. Nash's troubles are *my* doing, he told himself. I was a selfish idiot. I made no room for my own son, for Marek. If Marek is The Cold Fish, I am The Fish Maker.

"You know how long man lives?" Kaz asked.

"Till he dies?" Nash said.

"No. Man live as long as last person who know his story."

Kaz took a handkerchief from his back pocket, wiped his perpetually moist eyes.

"All people at Treblinka wanted to live. Life was not choice there. Choice is luxury. A gift. *Nash, you have choice.* Live for them. Live because they cannot."

Kaz put his hand on Nash's shoulder.

"I tell you now everything I remember about my tata and mama and sisters. You remember what I say. You live and tell. Tell your children. Tell *their* children. Keep little spark alive. Unlike you, we had no choice. We all died."

"Not you," Nash said, his eyes smiling.

"Yes, me too. Death is not just for the dead. I lay dead long time. Then I *choose* to live. I walk thousand miles and cross ocean to live."

Nash jumped down from the tailgate and hugged Kaz, pressed his face into the soft, loose skin of his grandfather's neck.

"I bring something," Kaz said. He took a shoebox from the truck's console and handed it to Nash.

"What's this?" Nash said. He opened the box and saw a motley, striped cap.

"My cap. From the camp."

"God," Nash said, half frowning. "Why'd you save it?"

"You keep it now. You are young. You have many years ahead. Things will be good. Things will be bad. Sometimes, terrible. When things are terrible, look at this. Look at this and see. Things are not so terrible."

* * *

Straddling the dirt bike, Evan took a firm grip around Nash's waist as they zipped across the teachers' parking lot at Tucker Elementary and rolled up onto Valley Way. Nash gunned his motorbike down Valley to Highway 61 and across the Raven Gorge Bridge. He felt Evan tighten his grip and hide his face when they shot across the gaping crack in the mountains. As they crossed the gorge and away from Cragmont—maybe forever—Nash tried not to think about his night on the bridge with The Bright Lady.

Instead, he thought about his plan to get Evan away from the drug holler, to teach him about the forest and bushcraft, backpacking and camping. Maybe fatten him up on GORP and oatmeal and cocoa. Nash talked to a lawyer about custody, but she said there wasn't a judge in the county who would consider a custody case, or even order a paternity test, given Nash's two stints at Hawthorne House. Evan would stay in foster care and be returned to Skeeter or Jett, whichever one slithered out of prison first.

Nash had deep, expert knowledge of Cragmont National Forest—especially the pristine PWZ, the federally protected wilderness zone—and was a volunteer on the county's Search and Rescue Squad. He'd logged a hundred miles in the national forest, searching for lost hikers. And maybe two hundred more on his own, rogue backpacking and camping miles off the official trails, breaking all the rules, looking for solitude and a place to quiet his mind—hiding, maybe, from a feared, inevitable return of The Bright Lady.

The PWZ's beauty and isolation, in particular, pulled at him. Eighty thousand acres with no logging roads or maintained hiking trails. No cell phone coverage, or even signs. It was a place for people with serious backcountry and map and compass skills. Casual nature geeks and weekend hikers were wise to keep out.

He'd lost track of how many waterfalls and deer and black bears he'd seen there over the years, so far from the nearest road he might as well have been on Neptune. Evan needed to see it, Nash decided, to learn there were good things in the world. And it was an ideal place to evade the local and state police who were probably looking for them in and around the town of Cragmont. Two days' head start, Nash figured, before authorities put two and two together and added the national forest to their search list.

Nash pulled off the highway onto Forest Road #9, a narrow gravel ribbon, and raced his bike twelve miles up the mountain to where it intersected with an abandoned dirt logging road that edged near the PWZ border. Five miles of barely passable road later, they hid the Suzuki in a ravine chock full of neck-high ferns and giant rhododendrons.

"Ever been camping?" Nash asked. Evan shook his head.

"You're going to love it." Nash uncovered the two backpacks he'd stashed there, holding water and snacks, map and compass and knife and all the other "ten essentials" anyone traveling across wilderness should carry.

They set off through the trailless woods, Nash leading the way and Evan right behind, eyes full of wonderment, gawking at the size of the trees and swallowed from time to time by thick green undergrowth taller than himself. They climbed further up the mountain for two hours and stopped for the night at a natural rock shelter, where erosion had carved a garage-sized gouge into a tall limestone outcropping. The rest of their supplies were stored there: a small backpacking tent, water filter, sleeping bags, winter clothing, and several weeks of dehydrated and packable food.

"We'll sleep here tonight," Nash said. It was twilight already. Evan took three or four tentative steps under the massive rock overhang, leaned against a boulder, and whimpered.

"It's safe here, no worries," Nash said. "Everything's fine."

Evan's face scrunched and reddened. He folded his arms and hung his head and began to cry in earnest.

The crying mortified Nash. "Hey, we've got Snickers!" he said. "And cocoa. You like cocoa, don't you? Sure, everybody does."

Nash dug around in his pack until he found his backpacking stove and little hockey-puck propane tank. He screwed the burner onto the tank and lit it up, put on a pot of water. By the time cocoa was ready, Evan had stopped crying but now lay on the ground, on his side in the dirt, arms around his knees.

"This'll cheer you up," Nash said, offering a tin cup of cocoa. Evan didn't look up.

"Hey, you know what else we brought?" Nash pulled out two magazines he'd rolled inside Evan's sleeping bag. "Motorcycles!"

Evan opened his eyes. Nash flipped the pages in front of Evan's face, the images dim in the waning light. He got the boy to sit up and fitted him with a headlamp, something the boy had apparently never seen. Evan sat on his rock sipping cocoa and carefully eyed every image on every page. Nash busied himself checking their gear and food until he heard the child slump to the ground again, asleep.

Near midnight, a full moon draped the forest in a ghostly, platinum light. Nash sat up rigid in his sleeping bag. There were footsteps cracking in the woods nearby, moving toward them. Nash grabbed his hunting knife, careful not to wake Evan. He crouched behind two of the larger rocks near the entrance of the shelter and unsheathed the knife, slowly raised his head to look.

A black bear. Must have caught scent of their dinner. Nash relaxed, let out a deep breath, and sheathed his knife. He shouted and clapped his hands. "Go bear! Go!" The bear froze for a moment before turning and diving back into the woodland night.

Nash chuckled.

Just a bear. I was afraid it was The Bright Lady.

At first light, the unmistakable bass thumping of a helicopter awakened Nash. It was crisscrossing the PWZ in a grid-search pattern.

"Shit," Nash said under his breath. He moved all their gear as far back under the rock ledge as he could. Evan tugged on Nash's sleeve and pointed at the sky.

"Helicopter," Nash said. "Looking for us." Evan grimaced and made fists with both hands and slapped his arms against his sides. Shook his head no. No. No. He pressed his face into Nash's bicep, gripped it with both hands.

This was not how Nash planned it. He was certain they would have two to three days to traverse the PWZ, climb over the top of Mt. Pickford, and down to Lake Stanway where he'd left his truck at a remote trailhead. From there, they'd drive the backroads to the boonies of eastern Kentucky, where he'd rented a cabin from one of the old-timer mountaineers who lived off-grid down there. Paid three months in advance. Cash. No names, no questions.

He doubted the chopper could get a line of sight on them, except from due west, unless they flew lower, which they eventually would. Too late to pack up and move into deeper tree cover without being seen.

"Dammit to hell!" Nash shouted and kicked his sleeping bag into the air, throwing up a haze of finely powdered dirt. Two hours, he told himself. Two hours before SWAT rappels down on us.

The boy covered his ears and cowered against the inner wall of the place. Nash chided himself for having scared the kid. He crouched down next to Evan and smoothed the boy's hair. Evan leaned against Nash, wrapped his arms around him.

"It's OK," Nash said. "We'll be fine."

Nash made Evan a breakfast of oatmeal, summer sausage, and cocoa. They sat together and scrutinized each and every bike in both magazines, with Nash explaining the different types of frames and engines and transmissions. Now and again, Evan pointed at one of the bikinied models draped over a motorcycle. Nash brushed off the questions at first, and finally said, "Oh, well . . . that's her bike. Guess she's going to ride it to the beach."

Evan waved his empty cup, and Nash promptly refilled it with cocoa. The copter rose through the valley between their shelter and the next mountain. The gut-wrenching, ill-wind noise of it funneling up the holler. Nash laid eyes on it for the first time, a glint of reflected sunlight, far down the mountain.

"Not long now," he said to himself.

He took a hand towel from his backpack. "Look," he said to Evan. Nash unrolled the towel and revealed a tattered, striped cap. Handed the cap to the boy. The child flipped it in his hands. Rubbed its odd, rough texture. He pointed at the cap and then pointed at himself, quizzically. Nash nodded. "Yours," he said. Evan smiled his rare smile.

"Evan," Nash said as the chopper passed high overhead. "Let me tell you about your great-grandfather. Kaz."

Late Fiction

THE WRITER

Vultures flock to the small town of Hobart, Ohio, every summer. They cover the trees with their dark, brooding silhouettes. They align themselves like a battalion of death sentries—fifty at a time—across the long, century-old slate crest of the Rickman Student Union building at Hobart State University, and stare. Some estimates say three thousand gather every year, maybe more. Ornithologists from across the world come to the rural college town of Hobart to study the phenomenon. All are mystified as to why it happens. Why here? Why at all?

I'm no ornithologist—I teach creative writing at HSU—but I know why the buzzards come. They come to pick the bones of my career.

My first novel, *Where the Ragged People Go*, was a finalist for the National Book Award. The second book, *Bridge to Everywhere*, won the Pulitzer for fiction. And my third (and last), that wretched pile of uninspired sentences and plot holes called *Rodeo Monkey*, hit Amazon like a turd hurled by . . . well, a monkey.

Everyone hated it: *The New York Times* ("shockingly mediocre"), *The Washington Post* ("frankly, an embarrassment"), elite critics and influencers, readers—especially fans of my other two books. My third wife (now ex), friends (also, now mostly ex), and family hated it—even if they didn't say so, a writer knows. I considered reading it to Cormac, the family dog at the time, hoping to at least get a few random tail wags, but then thought better of the idea. No need to add animal cruelty to my rap sheet of humiliation and failure. My crash was swift and painful, dropping from the English faculty of NYU (the top) to Boston College (respectable) to Texas Mid-State (embarrassing) to my current exile at HSU (literary Siberia).

If teaching in a place best known for vulture infestation was not degrading enough, I was being stalked by a seventy-something farmer. He'd written a novel. Yes, yes, of course he had. Apparently, every Ensure®-sucking, diaper-clad, titanium-hipped Boomer living within a two-hundred-mile radius of Hobart, Ohio, had written or was writing a novel. Or at the very least, a short story or ten. About their cat. Or how their tender, teenage heart was broken by the head cheerleader. Or the untimely death of *such-a-good-boy* Spiffy the childhood pup.

I had to read this shit because my boss, Dr. Hector Vicente, the chairperson of the English Department, had the brainstorm to create a badly needed new revenue stream for the university called "Late Fiction: The Hobart State University Senior Writers' Conference," held each summer and specifically designed for older people, age sixty-five and up. Three days of craft lectures, workshops, and one-on-one feedback sessions with geezer neophytes. Christ!

Most of these clowns, as they circle the drain and realize the meaninglessness of their lives—finding themselves sitting on fat-ass 401(k)s with nothing else to fill the hours—announce themselves "writers" with SOMETHING TO SAY. Few can string three good sentences together.

I didn't know if my stalker farmer could write a good sentence or not, and I wasn't going to know because, as I told him repeatedly, *"I'm not reading your novel!"* He attended the conference—having never submitted a writing sample—and somehow got the notion I would Yoda him along. Affirm his worth, his intellect, his stinking soul. Wrong guy, pal.

Hector saddled me with this mud-pig of a job so the university could plaster my long-faded accolades across the conference's website and brochures to impress all the grandmas and grandpas across flyover land: *Come one, come all! Come learn at the feet of novelist Preston Grant. Admire his Pulitzer. Learn how to catch a permanent case of writer's block. Watch him slowly dissolve into obscurity before your eyes!*

Very clever of Hector, finding a way to use me to put arthritic butts in chairs—at fifteen hundred dollars a pop—and at the same time punish me for his suspicion that I was sleeping with his wife, Lila. I was, but still, punish the crime before the indictment? Downright Un-American.

And that stalking farmer? He's why Lila and I got caught.

THE FARMER

I don't farm anymore. Don't do much of anything but slowly go blind. Age-Related Macular Degeneration (AMD). That's a diagnosis creative writing professors refer to as "the inciting incident" of a story. About a year ago, when the docs told me I was entering late-stage AMD and had maybe two years of functional vision left, it incited the hell out of me to get my novel published.

I started writing it as a nineteen-year-old infantry grunt in Vietnam in 1968. Carried the loose, handwritten pages in my pack where most soldiers carry a Bible or extra ammo or maybe letters from home. Maybe pictures of their honeys, or dope or porn. Little comforts to salve the nerves between alternating bouts of terror and boredom. Not me. I already knew the Bible front to back, and was on very good speaking terms with God. I didn't smoke or drink anything. Didn't have a girl back home.

My opiate was words, to bury myself in story, to let myself sink headlong into a self-induced trance, scribbling on any scrap of writable material I could find. The backs of maps. The backs of letters from my parents.

Candy wrappers or cardboard. Anything. Random notes at first. Then paragraphs that made little sense until I nipped and tucked and nursed them into complete pages that did.

The manuscript grew steadily, filling up more and more space, both physical and spiritual. It was scraggly and ragged, stained with coffee and greasy C-ration fingerprints, with sweat and blood, paddy water and piss. Ugly to look at, to be sure, but *my* ugly baby, beautiful on the inside I hoped, growing there in my pack, along for the murderous journey. The two of us traversing muddy swamps and deep bush. Surviving ambushes and napalm drops. My baby, gestating across a full tour of duty, right there in its little olive-drab womb strapped to my back. Miraculously intact—save for a shrapnel rip through the first forty pages—and about one-third complete when I left Nam in '69.

When I got home, Dad was too sick to harvest his crops, so I stepped in. Temporarily helping my parents out, I thought, then back to the novel. Dad died. The "helping" turned into owning and farming my parents'— mostly leased—five hundred acres of corn and soybeans, along with a second job selling used cars to make ends meet.

During those first few years back from the war, there would be times late at night when I managed a few new sentences, or maybe a handful of edits and revisions. But over time, those snippets of work petered out. What was the point of it after all? A foolish waste of time.

Decades clicked off, and I turned into a middle-aged man with a wife and two young children to feed and clothe with my patchwork of income from dirt-farming and hawking cars. The idea of walking into a bookstore, or even better, a library, and seeing my book under the same roof with O'Connor and Melville, Chabon and Atwood seemed more and more like childish, self-indulgent fantasizing.

One day I woke atop a steep pile of years and looked out to see my twenty-something self, toiling way down the mountain. I shouted to him and waved my arms and pointed. Pointed to the exact spot where his dreams would die.

THE WRITER

We broke out into genre groups, and I stood at the lectern in the classroom set aside for the fiction workshop and watched a dozen aspiring oldsters take their seats, many of them stutter-stepping down the aisles like heavily sedated sloths.

I knew Hector wanted me and my fellow colleagues to sing the same song, our national anthem of bullshit, cheerleading the seniors with "it's never too late." He'd plastered that slogan on all forms of tchotchkes to sell to them: T-shirts, notebooks, tote bags and backpacks, on and on ad nauseum. I wanted to bellow out to them as they took their seats:

"Oh, but it *is* too fucking late! You can't start writing now and accomplish anything worth a damn. Show some respect! This is not something you wait to do until you *have time* in your life, until you retire. It has to be your life *during* your life. This is not a hobby! Would anybody walk into a vanity basketball camp and expect to one day join the NBA? No one here is ever going to be LeBron James.

"Spend your last few years relaxing. Don't torture yourself. Do something fun. Cruise maybe. It takes decades of self-loathing, deprivation, and rejection to master the skills necessary to properly crush yourself with a keyboard."

That workshop was the first time I met the farmer. His name tag read "Carl Flanagan" and he had a pine-tree look to him—well over six feet, trim and tight with longish, wispy gray hair that shifted every time the air conditioner kicked on. He was the only one who hadn't submitted the "required" ten-page writing sample. Who was Hector kidding with that "required" bit? The university wasn't about to forgo fifteen hundred bucks over a missing ten pages of drivel.

"Mr. Flanagan," I said. "Did you not submit a writing sample? That means no one here has read your work. So we can't discuss it."

"I brought it with me," he said and lifted a disheveled, stained tome over his head.

"Holy crap," the woman behind him said. "Is that all handwritten?"

"Never learned to type," the farmer said, his voice scratchy and strained.

"Good grief, man," someone said. "Hire it out."

"Don't want to leave it anywhere," Flanagan said and looked down at his bundle. "It's the only copy. It means everything to me. I never let it out of my sight."

"Better find a Kinko's," someone in the back shouted. "Although that'd be a bitch to copy. One damn page at a time, I bet."

"OK, everyone," I said, trying to regain control of the room. "Mr. Flanagan, why don't you read us a few pages? Get some feedback that way?"

Flanagan shot me a startled look, then raked his eyes around the room. The class sat silent for a long moment while he fumbled for reading glasses, then pushed up from his chair and peeled back fat rubber bands from their death grip around the manuscript.

"Chapter one," he read and pulled the page to within a few inches of his face, then pushed it back and changed the angle. Criminy, I thought, he can't even read his own handwriting. Or worse, he can't read well, so how good could his writing be?

He muttered a few words at a time, almost in a whisper, often breaking mid-sentence to readjust the paper for better light. His wavering, shy voice and halting speech made it impossible to make much sense of what he was reading. About mid-way through the third paragraph, the farmer fell silent and clamped his eyes, trying but failing to block tears. He bowed his head and wiped his eyes on his shirt sleeve.

"Sorry," he said. "This gets a little emotional for me."

"Thank you, Mr. Flanagan," I said, ending everyone's misery. "That's enough for today. See all of you tomorrow morning."

THE FARMER

That first winter back from Vietnam, Dad was in bad shape. He'd had a massive heart attack a few months before I came home, and it kicked him into congestive heart failure. Systolic failure they called it, meaning his heart was damaged so much it could no longer properly pump blood through his body. He struggled to sit up in bed and spoke in a weak, gasping voice. Couldn't make it twenty feet to the bathroom and back without leaning against the wall to rest. He would probably live a few more years, the doctors told my mother and me—if he didn't have another heart attack or stroke—but there was no coming back from it. It would be all downhill now, probably not long before he would need full-time nursing home care.

This news turned my previously joyful, perpetually optimistic mother into a zombie. I'd awake to her wailing at three a.m. and run to her bed as she surfaced from a nightmare, sweating and shaking and pounding the headboard. This went on for a month until I finally got her to talk.

Over coffee one morning, she told me the farm was bankrupt, the mortgage on their modest house underwater, the annual lease payment on the land due soon. Their health insurance was lousy, covering some of Dad's expenses but still leaving them with major bills to pile on top of other bills. The mortgage could be covered for another couple of months by exhausting their savings, but there was otherwise no way out, nothing of significant value to sell, no way to raise cash.

"If we're evicted, I could move in with my sister, your Aunt Pauline, in Cincinnati," she said. "Get a job at McDonald's or something."

"What about Dad?" I asked.

"I can't ask Pauline to take both of us. Not in the shape your dad's in."

"Then what? A nursing home? God, those are awful places."

"You're young, Carl. I don't want you tangled up in all this. Your dad and I will figure it out."

"How would you even pay for a nursing home?" I asked.

"If we were destitute, he'd qualify at some facilities. The ones who get funding from the State or something, I think."

"Those places must be the worst of the worst."

"You should start looking for a regular job, Carl. Or maybe the Army has some benefits you could use for college?"

The idea of college did appeal to me. Hobart State was only ten miles away. I'd major in English and load up on creative writing courses. I'd learn to type and live in the library and work on my novel every day between classes. Read all the great books I always wanted to read. Go to bars and coffee houses and debate novels with literary folks. For the right people, I'd let them take a peek at my war-torn baby-in-progress. Maybe impress a few co-eds with my wordsmithery. Yeah, sure. Someday, far away.

"No way I'm leaving here and throwing the two of you to the wolves. I'll get another part-time job somewhere. Do whatever it takes to keep things afloat."

I showed Mom a half smile, but the words lay sour in my mouth. I didn't mind working hard; that's the way I was raised. But getting yet another job meant I'd never have time to work on my book. This was the trade-off God had given me: write a book no one will likely ever see, or help save my parents. It sounded like an easy choice. It wasn't.

*   *   *

The night my father died, snow collapsed the roof of the barn. I'd driven into Hobart to see a movie and buy feed, and when I returned, the barn was a pile of splinters and twisted tin roof panels, capped by a gigantic scoop of winter. I started digging out the tractor and as much other equipment as I could, to assess damages to the few pieces of property we had to sell. After an hour of shoveling, hands and feet numb and stiff, I trudged to the house to change into dry clothes. Got some coffee and sat by the fire. Let the quiet and the dark wash over me.

Mom was whimpering upstairs. She was in the master bedroom, where Dad's hospital bed was set up next to the regular bed.

"Mom? You OK?"

"Don't come in here!"

"Mom, what's wrong?" I pushed the door open a crack. She was slumped to the floor, her back against Dad's bed, a pillow in her lap.

"Why are Dad's arms tied down?" I asked.

"It's the best way, Carl," Dad said, not much above a whisper. Mom sobbed and clutched the pillow tighter to her body. Turned her head to the wall.

"Pills would show up in blood work," Dad said. "If there was an investigation."

"No—no. Jesus God!" I stomped over to Mom and snatched the pillow from her. "Have you both lost your minds?" I shouted.

I bent over, eye level with Mom. "Smother him?" I said, my voice cracking. She covered her face with her hands and wailed.

"Don't blame your mother," Dad said. "My plan. All the way. I've got enough life insurance to pay off the house. And there'd be a little left over for living expenses. For a short while, anyway. We'd default on the medical stuff. What're they gonna do, repossess me?"

"There's got to be another way," I said, trembling. I could always tell when he was serious about something. He had that distant, stony look in his eyes.

"There ain't," he said. "And the insurance won't pay if it's suicide. I'm sick as hell. Everybody who knows us knows that. Won't be no big whoop if I don't wake up one morning. We just have to make it look good."

I sat on the floor next to Mom and put my arm around her. She stopped crying and I started.

"I could live maybe two more years as an invalid, which would leave your mother homeless and penniless. I'll be goddamned if I go out that way."

Of course, Dad was right.

You're an asshole for even considering it; are the three of you God now?

It would solve a lot of problems, and it's coming soon anyway.

Mom keeps her house, and you get breathing room to write.

If I don't do it for them, they'll find another way—better me in prison than Mom, in case things go south.

OK, now you're making some sense.

Mom got to her feet, and I walked her downstairs. Poured a little Jim Beam in some coffee and set her up in front of the fire with her drink and a blanket. I took the Beam upstairs and when Dad saw it, he said, "Good idea." I poured him about two fingers.

"Carl, this ain't no church social. You better double or triple that."

I held the glass to his lips, and he drank it down. I hated the stuff, but I swallowed half a glass and checked how Mom had tied his arms to the bedsides, to make sure the padding was adequate. To make sure there'd be no bruising if he fought it, which was sure to happen.

I picked up the pillow and stepped toward him, and the tears came again. I covered my face. Cowardice had no place in the same room with his mettle.

"Son, you're a good man. I'm awful proud of you." He winked and gave me a wavering smile. I nodded.

He closed his eyes and took the deepest breath his failing heart and lungs would allow, then looked away for a moment, out the icy window. A full moon reflected off the snowbound, flat land he'd worked all his life, all the way to the horizon.

"Just think of it as finishing what God started," he said.

I raised the pillow, certain God was having none of it.

THE WRITER

I waited in my office for the farmer. It was time for his one-on-one feedback meeting with a real-life Pulitzer winner, although without a writing sample, I had no idea what we were going to talk about. Everyone was entitled to a short, private session each conference, but thank God only about half of them ever signed up. My waiting wasn't totally wasted though; I watched as two vultures pecked and ripped the windshield wipers off Hector's BMW.

I loathed the one-on-one meetings. They were the rotten rock bottom of the whole charade. Me, trapped face to face in a cramped office for fifteen minutes at a time with one sagging, faded bag-of-bones after another. I felt like the protagonist in a B-grade horror flick, awakening to discover I'd been sealed in a coffin with a corpse. A well-seasoned corpse.

That was it, the heart of my phobia. I was afraid of catching something from them. What? Frailty? Disintegration? Mortality? I was afraid of literally catching old age, and there was no cure for that, save death. I was Father Damien, wading through lepers, but without his grace and purity of soul. I didn't want to help the afflicted. I wanted to run like hell.

Oh, God did Jennifer Egan nail it when she said "time is a goon." A great big badass fucking goon—gonna mess you up, boy. Gonna mess you up good. And every damn summer, I get thrown smack into the middle of a major outbreak of the geriatric, time-goon virus.

It was four fifteen. The farmer was late. Only fifteen minutes left. Maybe he won't show.

I waited another five minutes before texting Lila a picture of the pink, padded handcuffs I'd bought. She texted me back a pic up her skirt.

Sorry, farmer. Got to go.

THE FARMER

My meeting with Professor Grant was at four o'clock, and I left in plenty of time.

As my vision worsened, I promised my kids I'd give up driving. But the two-lane country road from my house to the HSU campus was lightly traveled and only ten miles, a straight shot. I could see well enough to get there and back, the biggest problem being some fuzziness and blackness right in the center of my sight. I'd learned to work around that, but I knew time was running out. I needed to keep driving at least until the conference was over, until I could put my book in good hands. In Pulitzer-winner Preston Grant's hands.

About a half mile from campus, the car in front of me swerved around something I couldn't see. Buzzards. One of them smashed into my windshield, leaving it covered in a fractal maze of cracks and blood and buzzard shit, impossible to see through.

I left my truck on the shoulder and walked my novel the rest of the way into town, but it was too late. Professor Grant was gone.

THE WRITER

Lila and I had a system. She'd leave her and Hector's house to go for a run, then cut through the park to the bike path that passed right behind my place. About a mile total, but nothing for her—she was a marathoner. There was a thick strip of trees and brush between the back of my rental house and the bike path. A quick push through the undergrowth, and voilà. All she had to do was jump the back section of privacy fence that surrounded my yard—with the aid of some strategically stacked concrete blocks—and she had arrived.

Once inside the house, she'd usually shower, get a glass of wine, and then cuddle up with the two stray cats I'd taken in, Boo and Radley. There was nothing better than coming home to the three of them stretched out on the couch.

THE FARMER

I embarrassed myself the first day of workshop, breaking down while trying to read aloud from my book. I could blame it on diminished sight, which was partly the issue, but the truth was that in the reading of it to other people, I was seeing the true nature of the thing for the first time. And that both saddened and terrified me.

Standing there trying to read aloud, I was no longer in the twenty-first century, surrounded by well-to-do retirees in a safe, dry room. I didn't stand in a classroom in Hobart, Ohio. I stood in a burning Asian village in a past century.

The words seemed not my words but the ripped flesh of friends slaughtered in a forgotten war. The words were the broken bodies of dead children, the screams and pleas of dying teenage soldiers, and the last pale breaths I'd stolen from my father.

That stack of pages had ceased to be merely a story to me. It had become prayer and curse. An albatross formed by my own hand from the blood of warriors and the sin of patricide. Something to hold close and something to expel.

THE WRITER

The stalking began after the farmer missed his one-on-one opportunity. He ambushed me in the English Department's parking lot the next morning, foisting that nasty block of paper at me. I waved him off with "Sorry, sorry, no," repeated it a few times, faked a big smile, and almost broke into a run as I skirted past him and into the building. It was the last day of the conference. I figured that would be the end of it.

But no. He must have followed me from my office about a week later as I took a break. I sat in Roost Coffee, about half a block from campus, sipping a steaming Americano and texting Lila. When I saw him cross the street and head toward the cafe, manuscript under arm, I hightailed it through the tiny kitchen and into the back alley.

Over the next few weeks, he cornered me in the cereal aisle at Kroger. Drove up on me at a car wash. He'd lurk for hours in the hall outside my office, so I changed my office hours. I tried unsuccessfully to convince Hector I should move my office across the street into the History Building.

The farmer was relentless, I'll give him that. No amount of "sorry, no, can't help you, sorry, sorry, sorry" would work. "Sorry" became "Please go away" became "Just fucking leave me alone" became "I'm calling the police."

I didn't call the police. But I probably should have, because he somehow got my home address. That's when the real unraveling began.

THE FARMER

I wasn't proud of pestering Professor Grant, but damn it, he wouldn't take my phone calls or respond to letters. Talking to him in person was my only option, and time was running out on my ability to drive to HSU and back. If I could get just one hour with him, buy him drinks or dinner maybe, I'd convince him to read it.

If he liked it, maybe he'd talk his agent into taking a look. Spread the word among all the right people. And the truth was, I felt cheated because I only attended the Late Fiction conference to get that one-on-one meeting with him, and it was botched. I couldn't afford the fifteen-hundred-dollar tuition. Had to sell my Bronze Star, my grandfather's gold railroad watch, and Mom's one and only string of pearls to raise the money. All now wasted. I desperately needed to see that book in print, while I could still *see*. My book deserved to live.

I decided on one last try. Gave a kid in the HSU library twenty bucks to use one of the library's public computers to search the internet for Grant's home address.

No one answered the doorbell, and I couldn't see much from standing in the flower bed and peeking in the front window. It was a beautiful day. Maybe he was out back?

There was a tall privacy fence around the backyard, and the gate was unlocked. I went through and rounded the corner toward the deck, calling out "hello, hello," and almost bumped heads with Mrs. Grant. She was a striking woman with copper hair pulled back into a ponytail, wearing a black-and-tan yoga outfit and expensive running shoes.

"Jesus!" she said and jumped back, sucking in a deep, whistling breath.

"Oh, God!" I said. "So sorry. Didn't mean to scare you. I'm not a burglar—I promise. I'm a writer!" I smiled and held the manuscript up for her to see. "Just looking for your husband."

"You scared the bejesus out of me!" Her accent was British. Or maybe Australian. She jumped behind me and jerked the gate closed, but kept one hand on the pull.

"He's not here," she told me, annoyance in her voice. She took her phone from a holster around her bicep, paused, and rubbed her neck. Avoided eye contact with me. I prayed she wouldn't call the police.

"You best leave. Yes, that would be best." She opened the gate just enough for me to squeeze by.

"Yes, of course," I said. "Sorry I scared you."

The gate shut quickly behind me, and I heard the bolt clank into its slot.

THE WRITER

A week later, I stood on the English Department steps chatting with Khalid, one of our graduate assistants, when Hector and Lila came out of the building, headed for their car. We all said polite hellos as they passed. I tried not to make eye contact with Lila, which was our agreement if we ran into each other around Hobart. Khalid and I resumed discussing his MFA project when I heard the farmer's voice behind me.

"Hello, Mrs. Grant!" Flanagan said. "Again, I'm so sorry for scaring you in the backyard the other day. And I need to apologize to Professor Grant too."

I spun around to see what was happening. Lila froze and flashed a tense look up toward me.

"Vicente. My name's Vicente," she said. Flanagan narrowed his eyes, looked first at Lila, baffled, and then at Hector. An awkward pause later, he gave them a shallow nod, adjusted the grip on his manuscript, and headed up the steps toward me.

Hector leaned back and took a long look at Lila, like he was seeing his wife for the first time, then glared up at me. She tried to take his arm, but he jerked it back and sulked down toward the car, leaving her skittering along behind, calling out, "Hector . . . Hector. Wait!"

Enough was enough. I didn't care if the farmer was almost thirty years my senior; I was going to stomp him. I left Khalid behind and ran down to the old man and slapped that silly, mangy bundle out of his hands. It flew over the handrail and caught in the top of the hedges that grew eight feet high on either side of the concrete steps rising into the building.

"You're a goddamn idiot!" I yelled.

"Professor! Professor!" Khalid shouted, running behind me. "What are you doing?"

"No, no!" The farmer turned his back to me, fixated on his ridiculous manuscript. He leaned out for it, but it was just beyond reach, hanging by a twig or two above a long drop into the gunk and muck left by the sprinklers.

"Please God," he said, and laid himself belly out on top of the handrail, stretching.

"Sir, sir," Khalid called out to him. "Let me help you."

I climbed back up the steps as Khalid descended, planning my escape through the building, and hoping a twig would snap, and the damn thing would drop and fall and keep falling into the bottom pit of hell. *Get away from the old pest, Khalid, while you still have a chance. Save yourself!*

The farmer leaned further and further out. "Almost!" he cried, one hand on the railing, his other arm stretched past any natural limit. Khalid tried to grab the old man's belt, to belay him, but was a step too late. The farmer fell head first over the edge, both he and his novel vanishing into the bushes.

When the EMTs arrived, they said the shrubs apparently cushioned his fall a bit, but he'd still suffered serious neck and head injuries.

"At his age," one of the medics said, "he'll be very lucky to make it."

*   *   *

About midnight, Lila texted me she had confessed all to Hector, and they were staying together. That was it. I'd lost her. My untenured job at HSU, also gone. Hector would surely fire me tomorrow or the next day.

I sat in the dark on my patio, sipping Glenfiddich in a misting rain, trying to figure out how everything had collapsed over the past decade. Yeah, fired again. Next stop: teaching grammar at Inbred Community College in Bumfuck, Wyoming.

I drove to HSU, squinting through scotch goggles, navigating with one headlight because the other one was shattered when I hit a vulture three days ago. Disgusting creatures, like an army of grim reapers invading town.

I went to my office to get a head start packing my things, but also because my bottle had run dry, the liquor stores were closed, and I had another Glenfiddich locked in my desk. I flipped on the lights in my office and there sat the tattered mess of the farmer's manuscript square in the middle of my desk, waiting, patient as a rock. *Goddamn you, Khalid.* I picked it up to make sure I was really seeing what I was seeing, that the liquor hadn't fooled me.

Damn it was heavy. A rainbow of colors and a sampler of textures. I swear, some of the pages were written on the blank insides of chicken-feed sacks, rough cut to about letter size. I gulped whiskey and sniffed the little bitch. It stank. An odor like a cross between mildew and despair.

As I flopped it back down on the desk, the first line caught my eye. A brilliant opening. At least the old man's handwriting was legible. I read another line and then another. I was half sloshed, but I'd done some of my best analysis and thinking while sloshed. And some of my worst.

It was titled *Of Fathers & Gods*, and the slimy bastard hooked me from the first sentence, I mean hooked me right through the jawbone. Writ large, it was a retelling of the Old Testament story of Abraham and Isaac. His prose was beautiful. Lyrical but never pretentious. The structure was magnificently executed, the intertwining of two primary storylines. On one level, it was about a Special Forces colonel during the Vietnam war who struggles with the decision to send his own son on a suicide mission into a treacherous Viet Cong tunnel. But on another level, it was a recasting of the story, where America is Abraham, Vietnam is Mount Moriah, and 58,220 Americans are Isaac. But this time no angel arrives at the last minute to stay the hand of the father. Abraham completes the sacrifice of Isaac and waits in silence for God to approve.

By dawn I'd finished it, after taking several breaks to cry, or sit in stunned silence and ponder an especially striking section, a pitch-perfect chapter. It needed a few edits, of course, but the farmer's novel was the best thing I'd read in twenty years. The bad news was, it beat my three books all to shit. The good news, it set my mind on fire with ideas for a new book, a really good one, my comeback novel! I could see most of my new book in a single flash of imagination, just like my best days before *Rodeo Monkey*. At the exact moment I needed a lifeline, here it was. Steal from it? Oh, hell no. I might have been an asshole, but I was no plagiarist.

Shortly after sunrise, as I let the farmer's book seep further into me, I carried the crazy patchwork of pages down to the English Department's copy room. I couldn't stop sobbing over the beauty of it, and how it would change my life. No one is ever alone after falling in love with a great book.

I stood in the copy room and let tears of tribute and release flood over it as I peeled off a few pages at a time, and fed them into the shredder.

*   *   *

Hunched over an untouched Grand Slam breakfast at Denny's, I drank a river of coffee until I felt at least half sober, and decided that if the farmer survived, I'd tell him his manuscript somehow got mixed up with the trash. After all, it looked like trash. *So terribly sorry, but it's gone. Damn those janitors! Or damn those airheaded office people! You just can't get good help these days.*

As I sobered, my focus returned to the new book I had to write. I ordered a fresh carafe of coffee and ferociously jotted notes in my Moleskine. I rushed to get the broad strokes of plot down on paper before they floated away.

There would be two primary characters in conflict: a washed-up novelist turned misanthropic professor of creative writing who hates old people because they are harbingers of his own death, and an aged farmer with brilliant but undiscovered writing skills who sacrifices his literary dreams for the good of his family.

The farmer was in the ICU at Hobart-Stratton Memorial. I drove over there, as it was my habit to visit as many of the physical places as possible where scenes from my novels took place—the best way to get the details right, to make sure things rang true.

"Are you family?" the duty nurse asked, not bothering to look up from his computer.

"His nephew," I said. "Just flew in from California."

"Fifteen-minute limit on visits. There's some family in there now, so please wait in the hallway. Don't crowd the room."

"How's he doing?" I asked. The nurse said nothing, just looked at me and bit his lower lip. Shook his head.

I moved quietly toward the farmer's room and hovered in the hall, feeling like just another vulture come to town. There were two couples with him, about my age, and four children. All quiet but for an occasional muted comment or whisper.

I sat on a bench in the hall, just outside his door, checking messages on my phone.

"Excuse me," someone said. I turned and saw a fortyish woman leaning out from the farmer's room. She had a flat, round face and sandy-blonde hair, cropped short.

"Are you here to visit Carl Flanagan?" she said, her eyes moist and bloodshot.

What now? I had foolishly thought I could avoid talking to anyone. I tried to smile and opened my mouth to speak, but couldn't quickly think of just the right lie.

"Were you a friend of his?" she asked. "My father?"

"Yes," I said, standing, regretting I didn't have a clever answer, something to extract me from the situation. "He was just at my house. Maybe a week ago."

"Please join us," she said, and motioned toward the room. I looked up and down the hall, stalling, trying to think of some reason to say no. Couldn't come up with one.

As I entered, everyone turned and looked, nodding and sad-smiling at me.

"There's no brain activity," his daughter said to me under her breath. "They're going to remove life support today. After we leave."

"So sorry," I whispered.

"Let's pray," one of the men said. His son, I guessed.

Everyone stepped up to the bed, put their bodies right up against it, and held hands. A young girl to the right of me, maybe thirteen, grabbed my hand and pressed herself to the bed, but I hung back a step or two, stretching my arm as far as I could without breaking her grasp. A boy of nine or ten grabbed my other hand and pushed his chest up to the bed. He tugged at me—gently at first, then more aggressively—until I too had my thighs against the bed, just inches from his brain-dead grandfather.

I hadn't prayed since childhood, but bowed my head with his family and listened carefully to the words his son spoke, asking that Carl Flanagan be forgiven his sins, and his soul be folded into the eternal love of Heaven. The prayer done, they took turns leaning down to him, whispering last words, kissing his cheek or forehead. A gospel song broke out, low and sweet and salted with easy tears. An old favorite of his.

The sincerity of their love shocked me, as if an assailant had plunged a long, thick icicle into my chest. Shake it off, I told myself. Shake it off and focus on your book. But I couldn't.

Breaking away from the kids, I rushed into the hall and called my daughter for the first time in months. It went straight to voicemail. Tried to call my son, but apparently his number was no longer in service. I'd had no notice of that. He was a freshman at Boston University. Or was he a sophomore? I wondered if he was even still there? Most desperately, I called Sheila, my second wife, my favorite, but panicked and hit "cancel" when it began ringing.

Unlike me, the farmer had never been alone. He was not alone now. I could still feel his grandkids' hands in mine, could feel their grief and loss lingering on my skin. I dropped the phone and heard the screen shatter with a sickening crackle.

My grandkids, if any are born, will never know me like that. I doubled over on the bench and sobbed, struggled to keep myself under control, then finally lost it entirely, heaving and howling like a lost dog. I let the tears flow and covered my face in shame. The farmer's family filed out of the room, and almost to a person, reached down to hug me, to pass along a comfort, a little love.

"We're all going to miss him," his daughter said, and patted my shoulder. "You two must have been great friends."

*   *   *

With the family gone, I went back in the room and sat at the foot of his bed, expecting medical people to show up at any moment to pull the plug. I sat there a long while, sniffling and wiping my nose. Thinking about how he was loved. Thinking about how I traded three wives and two kids for a Pulitzer Prize.

"Sorry for shredding your book," I said to the dead farmer. "I was drunk. No, I was jealous. And, I was really pissed off about Lila. OK, you're right, all of the above. Alcohol, women, and jealousy. That's always a bad cocktail."

I sat in the little half-glass room and took it all in. The sounds, smells, colors. How his gown draped on his body, a count of the tubes and wires, their colors and locations. The angle of the bed, how the window blinds hung askew, the odd speckled nature of the floor. Then I began pouring notes into my Moleskine, capturing the details, trying to refocus myself on the new book I had to write.

I always started a new piece of fiction with two things in mind: the title and the ending. I'd title the new book *Of Fathers & Gods*, not as plagiarism—titles can't be copyrighted anyway—but as homage to the farmer's book, as a way of bringing a little of his novel back from the shredder.

And in a way, I could bring *him* back as well. Yes, this scene here, this was it: the ending for my comeback novel, my ticket back to civilization. So, from the foot of my newest protagonist's death bed, I put these words into his mouth:

Look at the professor, pitying me because I teeter on the abyss. He wonders what my life was like, if I fought with monsters, wonders how far the abyss looks into me. He knows I'll never walk into a bookstore or library and see myself alongside all the other narcissists. Never see my name on a book spine, that marquee of confirmation, sitting pretty on a shelf. Knows I'll never see my name over someone's shoulder, centered in the glow of a screen, one click away from a new sycophant, a new stranger to inspect my heart and judge my humanity.

I never had any of those things, because I couldn't sacrifice the love of other humans to play God with ink and paper. But I had what the professor will never know. The invincible love of a wife and children, the love of one's children being the only true way to touch the future.

Dear Professor, you and I have done the saddest of dances, each seeking the other's treasure, each blind to his own.

Acknowledgments

The author wishes to thank the following publications and fiction competitions for first publishing or honoring earlier versions of the following stories:

"While Her Guitar Gently Weeps," *Prime Number Magazine*
    Pushcart Prize Nominee
    Runner Up, *Prime Number Magazine* Award for Short Fiction
    Quarterfinalist, ScreenCraft Cinematic Short Story Competition

"Pocketknife," *Flash Fiction Magazine*

"Tender, Like My Heart,"
    Finalist, ScreenCraft Cinematic Short Story Competition

"The Jackshit Bastards," *Rappahannock Review*
    Finalist, ScreenCraft Cinematic Short Story Competition

"Late Fiction," *ArLiJo, The Arlington Literary Journal*

My first thanks go to Donna Berry (Roberts) for jumping off a cliff with the eighteen-year-old me and free falling fifty years into the people we've become. I can't find words fancy enough or powerful enough to convey adequate gratitude for the oceans of love, support, and emotional sustenance you have provided to keep me alive all this time. You are always my first reader and I'm convinced I'd have never published a word without you.

Big thanks to our sons, Mark and Adam Roberts. First, for not rushing me to a mental facility after reading early drafts of my stories, and second, for taking time from very full lives to read and ponder, and in so doing, improve my writing.

Gratitude to Mrs. Betty Lunsford, my Honors English teacher senior year in high school, for indulging my request to add creative writing to her lesson plans (much to the dismay of my classmates), and for slipping me a couple of banned novels to further stoke my interest in fiction. Wish you were still with us to sneak this book to the right someone because I'm sure it'll be banned somewhere.

A salute goes to John Matthew Fox who provided critical developmental editing support for every story in this book. An award-winning author, he is also a fiction surgeon, using his X-ray vision to show me where the broken bones and tumors lie in my work, and always prescribing the perfect literary medicines.

Speaking of fellow writers, I'd be remiss not to send out thanks to my cross-country Zoom-powered writers' group, CINCO. The time and effort this talented group of writers put into reviewing and critiquing my work is greatly appreciated. By name, they are:

Mary Hester

Georgia San Li

Cynthia Nooney

Jasper Rine

Mike Saeugling

Many, many years ago I was fortunate enough to have met—and received some brief but invaluable long-distance mentoring from— Gail Galloway Adams (West Virginia University) and Chuck Kinder (University of Pittsburgh), both writers and fiction educators. Gail Adams put many hours into reading and critiquing the raw draft of a novel I'd written, and I greatly appreciate that selfless, unpaid act, and for the fact she miraculously saw enough good things in it to encourage me to keep writing. I will also be forever grateful to Chuck Kinder for convincing me I wasn't wasting my time pursuing writing, and for teaching me my mantra: *Fiction is Trouble.* May he rest in peace.

And heartfelt appreciation to Casie Dodd, founder and publisher at Belle Point Press, for seeing merit in these stories and publishing this debut collection, turning my dream into reality.

JIM ROBERTS grew up in rural East Texas. After college, he lived and worked briefly in Houston before moving to Cincinnati, Ohio, in the early 1980s to pursue a business career. Now a full-time writer, he and his wife, the artist Donna Berry Roberts, split their time between Ohio and Texas, depending on whim, changes in the weather, or the beckoning of distant haints.

His fiction has appeared in *Prime Number Magazine, Rappahannock Review, Snake Nation Review, Flash Fiction Magazine,* and *The Arlington Literary Journal* (*ArLiJo*). His work has been nominated for a Pushcart Prize and twice named to the finalist list for the Screencraft Cinematic Short Story Award.

Learn more at **jimrobertsfiction.com**.

Belle Point Press is a literary small press
along the Arkansas-Oklahoma border.
Our mission is simple: Stick around and read.
Learn more at bellepointpress.com.